Dear Reader,

I'm a huge reality TV fan. I don't watch all the shows, but I do have my favorites. Some of which you may be able to tell when you read this story.

The idea for this book came after watching the finale of a reality dating show, complete with diamond engagement ring and romantic proposal. I couldn't stop thinking, What if the man proposed to the wrong woman?

Enter Millie Kincaid and Jace Westfall—two people who aren't ready for each other the first time they meet, but who get a second chance!

I loved creating my own reality TV show. The race around the world for a million dollars takes place in eight different countries, so this was the most research I ever had to do for a book. I spent many hours searching settings, flights, and weather, along with activities the characters could do during each race leg, so they not only grew as individuals, but became a couple and fell in love. I also got to watch my favorite reality shows and call it research!

I hope you enjoy reading about Millie and Jace as they set out to win the race—and each other!

Sincerely,

Melissa

With a degree in mechanical engineering from Stanford University, the last thing **Melissa McClone** ever thought she would be doing was writing romance novels. But analyzing engines for a major U.S. airline just couldn't compete with her happily-ever-afters. When she isn't writing, caring for her three young children or doing laundry, Melissa loves to curl up on the couch with a cup of tea, her cats and a good book. She enjoys watching home-decorating shows to get ideas for her house—a 1939 cottage that is *slowly* being renovated. Melissa lives in Lake Oswego, Oregon, with her own real-life-hero husband, two daughters, a son, two lovable but oh-so-spoiled indoor cats and a no-longer-stray outdoor kitty that decided to call the garage home. Melissa loves to her from her readers. You can write to her at P.O. Box 63, Lake Oswego, OR 97034, U.S.A., or contact her via her Web site: www.melissamcclone.com.

MELISSA MCCLONE
Win, Lose...or Wed!

HARLEQUIN®

TORONTO • NEW YORK • LONDON
AMSTERDAM • PARIS • SYDNEY • HAMBURG
STOCKHOLM • ATHENS • TOKYO • MILAN • MADRID
PRAGUE • WARSAW • BUDAPEST • AUCKLAND

ISBN-13: 978-0-373-03995-1
ISBN-10:   0-373-03995-6

WIN, LOSE...OR WED!

First North American Publication 2007.

www.eHarlequin.com

Printed in U.S.A.

Melissa McClone on *Win, Lose...or Wed!*:

"While much of this story takes place in exotic settings that required research, Millie and Jace begin their adventure in San Francisco, where I used to live. Like my heroine, I'm not fond of heights. She, however, makes it to the top of Coit Tower. I never did."

For Tom, Mackenna, Finn and Rose

Special thanks to:

Colin Goldstein, Michael Leming, PortlandHikers.com,
Terri Reed, Tiffany Talbott & Virginia Kantra

PROLOGUE

"Two more minutes, Millie."

Oh, boy. Millie Kincaid shivered. It was almost time.

She glanced at the gilded framed full-length mirror hanging on the wall of an opulent mansion in Pacific Palisades, California. She barely recognized her reflection. The curly updo, the professionally applied makeup and the elegant gown made her look like a princess, not a schoolteacher from a small town in Central Oregon.

She felt a little like Cinderella. Not that Millie needed an invitation to the ball to find her Prince Charming. She'd already found him on a reality television show, no less. Her heart beat faster. She just had to get through the show's final episode tonight when "The Groom," Jace Westfall, a money manager from Philadelphia with his own company, would pick his bride.

An aviary worth of butterflies fluttered in Millie's stomach. She couldn't believe she'd made it to the finale. She'd only attended the show's audition so her friend wouldn't have to go alone. Her father, a successful motivational speaker, who didn't think she was living up to her potential, told her she wasn't ready for a show like this, and she'd wondered if he were right.

Until meeting the handsome "Groom" and falling for him.

Despite the certainty in her heart that she'd found the "one," she wasn't expecting an engagement ring after only knowing each other a few weeks. What she really wanted was time alone with him, away from the cameras, crew and other contestants. How would they get along when it was only the two of them? Her head told Millie counting on forever was nothing more than a teenage fantasy. Yet, in her heart, she couldn't help believe she'd glimpsed her future in his eyes.

"Millie?" Avery, a young production assistant, adjusted her headset. "Are you ready?"

"Yes." Millie stepped over cables running along the inlaid wood floor, teetering on the crystal-encrusted high heels they'd given her to wear, and ignored the bright lights and cameras focused on her. She straightened. "I'm ready."

Grinning, Avery clutched a clipboard to her chest. "You look so beautiful. Just wait until Jace sees you. He's going to love you."

Millie hoped so.

I never thought I'd find someone like you on this show.

Jace's words, murmured in her ear after a good-night kiss, sent anticipation rippling through her.

"Well, I think he knows the real me." Jace saw beyond Mousy Millie, the nickname given by her father when she was an awkward, shy teenager, to the woman she really was inside. Jace asked questions about her job as a special education teacher and listened to her answers. He wanted to know her thoughts, her opinions, her dreams. He talked with her, not at her. As joy overflowed, Millie motioned to her fancy hair and beautiful dress. "The rest is window-dressing."

"Which is why you were selected the viewers' bride

choice on the show's Web site. You and Jace are the perfect couple. Right up there with the ultimate reality couples Trista and Ryan and Amber and Rob." Avery sighed. "And you are beautiful. So accept the compliment and say thank you."

Millie's cheeks warmed. "Thank you."

She appreciated Avery's kind words, but she couldn't help wondering how beautiful her competition, Desiree Delacroix, a mortgage broker from New York, would look. The other bride finalist exuded strength, confidence and raw sex appeal. Desiree had no problem wearing a string bikini or just a towel in front of Jace and the cameras. Millie would rather face an entire class of kids sick with the stomach flu than wear a swimsuit on television. She'd chosen Whistler, B.C., as her final date location instead of Cancún, Mexico, to avoid wearing skimpy clothing. Two women couldn't have seemed more different, yet they shared a love of children, a belief in the institution of marriage…and an attraction to Jace Westfall. Thinking about their similarities and differences made Millie squirm.

The set went quiet, as if someone had hit the mute button. Avery touched her earpiece. "It's time."

Every one of Millie's nerve endings sprang to life. Excitement surged. She couldn't wait to see Jace.

She walked through the mansion, accustomed by now to ignore the equipment, the cameras and the crew. The show's host, who also worked on the network's nightly entertainment news show, gave her the thumbs-up. He'd interviewed her when she first arrived. Now it would only be her and Jace. And the cameras.

Rounding the corner to the final set, she saw him, standing on a balcony with hundreds of flowers. Jace wore a black tuxedo with a red rose boutonnière pinned on his lapel. He seemed taller, almost larger than life, all dressed up and his light brown hair neatly styled. This was how he would look on his wedding day. She sucked in a breath.

His eyes widened when he saw her. Uh-oh. He looked almost...scared. Her heart went out to him. This was a big moment for both of them. Millie fought the urge to run and reassure him the way he had that first night on the show when the world of reality TV had threatened to overwhelm her.

But before she could reach him, he smiled. At her.

Suddenly all was right in the world. In Millie's world.

The backdrop of the Pacific Ocean stretching to the horizon brought out the blue in his eyes. She couldn't help but wonder if they had children whether their babies would have his eye color or green like hers. Maybe hazel.

No, she was getting ahead of herself. But that was part of his appeal. He might be strong and solid, but he also made her loosen up and want to take chances. When Jace was around, her dreams became possible. She loved that about him.

If they had children someday, Millie hoped the kids inherited Jace's smile. She loved his wide, easy smile. Not to mention the determined set of his jaw and the little bump on the center of his nose. He was so handsome, so supportive, so caring.

Contentment coursed through her. The way his gaze never left hers made Millie feel cherished and adored. She seemed to be floating, even though she knew that was physically impossible. Unless a fairy godmother had waved a magic wand.

Millie wouldn't be surprised. The balcony defined romance with the elegant flowers and flickering candles everywhere. Music—Pachelbel's Canon in D—played from hidden speakers while waves crashed against the shore below.

A breeze ruffled Jace's hair. A strand fell forward across his forehead, making him seem appealingly real and approachable.

Even though she knew the killer setting was as carefully contrived as her appearance tonight, Millie found herself totally caught up in the mood. The moment. The magic.

She moved toward him. The scent of roses, her favorite flower, wafted in the air. She caught a scent of salt, too, blowing off the ocean. Millie wanted to etch every detail on her brain so she wouldn't forget anything. Of course, she would be able to watch the scene over and over again. That was one good point of the show, a visual recording of their falling in love.

Millie stopped in front of him. "Hi."

"Hi, Freckles." His appreciative gaze started at the top of her head and went down to the tips of her oh-so-out-of-her-budget sling backs. "Though I don't see many freckles tonight. You look amazing."

Okay, relenting and allowing the production staff to do her hair, makeup and clothing for tonight's show had been a good thing after all. She kind of liked looking and feeling like a princess. Millie wiggled her toes.

"Stunning," he added.

His words wrapped around her heart like a warm hug. "Thanks," she said. "You, too. Stunning. I mean, handsome."

"Millie." Smiling, he reached toward her and his large hands engulfed hers. "My sweet Millie."

This was it. Her pulse quickened. She wanted to hear him say that he chose her. That he wanted her.

"Being with you has made these past few weeks fly by."

His warm voice, his words, resonated with her. "You always had an encouraging word or a smile for me. I don't know how I would have made it through without you."

"Me, either."

"We had so much fun together."

Remembering all the good times, Millie nodded. Those were only the beginning. They had a lifetime of memories to create together. A lifetime. She nearly sighed.

He looked at their linked hands. "You became my confidant, my counselor, my good friend. I'll always value our friendship."

Friendship? Anxiety spurted through Millie. Okay, don't overreact. A relationship, not to mention marriage, needed a strong foundation that friendship provided.

Jace squeezed her hands. The action gave her no comfort. Zero reassurance. She needed him to say she was his choice.

His gaze returned to hers. "But you deserve someone better than me, Millie."

Oh, no. He can't be serious.

She searched his face for a sign to contradict his words, but found...nothing except for a fleeting look of regret in his eyes. A vise gripped her heart. She couldn't breathe.

"You need someone who will love you the way you should be loved." Jace said the words as if he were doing this for her own good. "I can't do that. I just...can't."

Millie heard a gasp. She wasn't sure if it came from her or one of the crew. It didn't matter.

She wanted to run away, but her feet remained cemented to the balcony. She opened her mouth to speak, but closed it. What was she going to say?

I can't do that.

His words reverberated through her body. Her eyes stung, but she was too numb to know if she was crying or not.

"I'm sorry if I hurt you," Jace said, his eyes dark. "I never wanted to do that, Millie. I really do…like you."

Like. Not love.

He didn't love her. He didn't want her.

The truth hit fast and hard like a javelin aimed right at her heart. Millie wrapped her arms around her stomach, trying to quell a rush of nausea.

Jace had never said he loved her. She'd known he'd kissed Desiree, too, but Millie had thought… She'd believed…

She had been wrong. About every moment they'd spent together. About every kiss they'd shared. About everything she thought she knew about Jace Westfall.

She'd been duped. Used. Dumped.

And she merrily went along.

Innocent. Naive. Stupid.

Millie turned away from Jace. She forced her feet to walk off the romantic set. Ignoring the cameras focused on her, she hoped someday to be able to forget the looks of pity on the crew's faces.

Never again. Millie left the mansion and stepped into an idling limousine. She would never let someone do this to her again.

CHAPTER ONE

Six months later...

HADN'T she learned her lesson the first time?

Standing on the granite plaza of San Francisco's Union Square with the statue of the goddess Victory looming over her, Millie couldn't believe she was doing this again. She shifted from foot to foot, trying to tap down her nervousness. She needed to pay attention to Pete Kenner, producer of *Cash Around the Globe,* the reality TV show she'd agreed to appear on.

Appear?

That's what the casting director had called it, but if things went Millie's way, she would spend the next thirty days racing around the world with a cameraman and sound guy at her side. Anxiety crept down her spine.

You know they will want you to jump out of an airplane or climb a mountain. Neither of which you have the courage to do.

Her father's words rushed back. He'd called her a coward, saying she was too soft and introverted to compete let alone win. What if he was right?

"You can only use the credit card for air travel," Pete explained. With his coiffed blond hair, tanned skin and smart clothing, he looked more like a model in *Maxim* than the head honcho for the network's most promising new show. "You will purchase tickets for yourself and your camera crew. You must remain with your crew at all times—24/7. Attached at the hip. Unless you use the rest room or shower."

Did rain showers count? Millie wondered. Mist pelted her cheeks, the dreary June weather adding to her growing apprehension. Doubts surfaced. Her father had predicted she would be the first one eliminated. She could easily make as big a fool of herself on this show as on…

Stop.

Think positive. Be confident. She could do this.

She would prove her father wrong.

So what if she had vowed never to step in front of another television camera again? Millie wasn't a reality TV contestant junkie. She was only doing the show to help her students at Two Rivers Elementary School. Whatever money she won would go directly to her school to keep upcoming budget cuts from affecting the students. The show's participation fee had already saved the after school track and field program she'd founded and coached for special needs students. That alone made up for whatever the show put her through over the next month.

And if she kept saying the words over and over again, she might come to believe them.

As Millie zipped her fleece-lined blue windbreaker to the top, she tried to remember her cameraman's name. Zack? Zeke? And her sound guy. Ron? Maybe Ryan?

Names usually stuck with her, but right now her mind was as blank as a chalkboard on the last day of school. Not a good thing when the two guys would be filming and recording everything she said and did.

"Bathroom breaks won't give us a lot of privacy," an older woman said. Her jacket resembled Millie's except for the orange color. Each contestant had been assigned a color and given clothes to wear during the race. Even their backpacks, lying on the other side of Union Square, coordinated to their colors.

Pete's bright white teeth contrasted with his dark tan. "There's no such thing as privacy on a reality television show."

Millie caught herself nodding. She didn't want to appear to be a know-it-all even if she was the only former reality TV contestant on the show.

A passing car honked its horn. Men in three-piece suits and women in raincoats stared at the lights and cameras. A construction worker yelled, asking if they were filming the new season of *The Amazing Race*.

No. Oh, no. That was one show she wouldn't want to be on. Relying on a partner, a teammate, to win or lose didn't appeal to Millie in the slightest. *Cash Around the Globe* would be different. Better. Or she would never have agreed to do it.

"Any questions?" When no one spoke up, Pete clapped his hands. "Let's get this show on the road."

Millie took a deep breath, the cold June air chilling her lungs. Goose bumps prickled her arms and legs.

A red light glowed on the cameras. Show time. She pasted on a smile, resigning herself to the role she would play until she was eliminated from the race or crossed the finish line.

Colt Stewart, with war correspondent good looks and a charming smile, stepped forward. "I'm going to be your host during the race around the globe. Are you ready for the adventure of a lifetime?"

"Yes," Millie said along with the other contestants.

"I didn't hear you," Colt said. "Are you ready for the adventure of a lifetime?"

The contestants shouted a hardy, "Yes!"

Colt flashed an even wider toothpaste ad smile at the cameras. "Welcome to *Cash Around the Globe*. This is the most exciting, most adventurous, most dangerous race you'll see on television. You won't want to miss a single episode."

By the time the race finished airing next season, her life would—she crossed her fingers—be back to normal. No more marriage proposals from strangers. No more early morning phone calls from talk show hosts. No more reality TV.

"Racers, prepare yourself," Colt yelled.

The contestants around Millie postured themselves for the best possible start. She did the same. A clanging rang out, the sound of a cable car bell. *Ding. Ding. Ding.*

"Go," Colt shouted.

Two guys, one in black, the other green, sprinted to the line of backpacks. Millie ran after them, adrenaline rushing through her veins. She would not fall behind. All the softness had been driven out of her. She was ready this time.

Ten feet from her blue backpack, she noticed a round zippered pouch with a globe imprinted on the front. Inside she found thirty dollars and a small key on a chain and a clue card.

"Make your way to Coit Tower," Millie read for the camera's sake. "You must travel via public transportation. Look for the green and blue flag. There you will find your next clue and something to take with you on the race."

Take with her? Her excitement swelled. A GPS unit would be great. Useful. Millie reread the clue.

"Coit Tower?" She'd never been to San Francisco before, but had heard of the landmark. Heart pounding, she surveyed the buildings around her. High-end department stores, boutiques and hotels. She saw a uniformed security guard and ran to him. "Could you please tell me where to catch the bus to Coit Tower?"

The guard led her to the bus stop. "Take the 30 or 45. Grab a transfer ticket when you board. Get off at Washington Square. Take the 39 to the top of Coit Tower. You can walk, if you'd rather, but it's a steep climb."

"Thank you," she said as the 30 bus pulled to the curb with a squeal of breaks.

The bus passed through Chinatown and North Beach also known as Little Italy. At Washington Square, she transferred to bus number 39 and rode to the top of Telegraph Hill. She exited. The camera crew followed her.

Tourists milled about the base of Coit Tower, snapping pictures. Not even the overcast skies could detract from the lovely view. Millie searched for a flag, but came up empty. She hurried up the steps to the tower's entrance.

Inside the circular lobby, Millie found colorful murals, but no clue box. That meant she had to go up. She disliked—okay, hated—heights, but purchased three tickets from the gift store anyway. With the camera crew and two students from Brazil, she crammed into a small elevator.

At the top, the doors opened, and everyone spilled out. She climbed a winding staircase to the upper viewing area. A breathtaking panoramic view of jutting skyscrapers greeted her through arched windows, but she stayed far away from the edge.

Millie stared for a moment feeling so much like a small town girl in the big city. And then she remembered…the race. Self-preservation kicked in. She located a blue and green banner flapping in the breeze.

"There's the clue box." A lock, however, kept her from opening it. "Good thing I have a key."

Millie stuck her key in the hole, but the lock wouldn't open. She tried again. "Why isn't this working?"

She took a closer look. "Two holes."

Millie inserted her key in the other hole. No luck. Fear pulsed through her veins. If she couldn't open the box to get a clue, she would be eliminated. Over her dead body.

Leaving the key in the lock, she examined the clue box. "What am I missing?"

"This," a male voice said from behind her.

She turned. A dangling silver key caught her attention. Millie focused on the man holding it.

Jace Westfall.

The air rushed from her lungs. No. He couldn't be here. With her. Now.

She felt wobbly, off-kilter as if she were standing on the top of a mountain or a tall tower that, Millie realized, she was. She struggled to breathe, but managed only a few gasps of air.

Falling.

That's all she could think about.

She was going to fall. Fail. Again.

Millie thought she had prepared for everything. But not for this. No way could she have prepared for this. For him.

"What are you doing here?" Her voice sounded ragged. Well, she felt ragged. But losing control would only give the show what they wanted. Drama. Obviously they had arranged for Jace to meet her here.

He waved the key. "Bet this opens the lock, Freckles."

Millie winced at his use of the endearment. She couldn't answer. She didn't want anything to do with him. If he were the last man on Earth, she would gladly die a virgin. She gnawed on the inside of her mouth.

A second cameraman, one she didn't recognize, moved closer.

She wrapped her arms around her stomach.

"You okay?" Jace asked quietly with a quick concerned look.

Millie wished he'd stop pretending. His compassion was nothing more than an act. He only cared about how he would be portrayed on camera. She wouldn't be taken in by his good looks and charm again.

Yes, she might have been heartbroken the night of the Groom finale, but she'd quickly realized everyone had gotten carried away on the show. Nothing, not even her feelings, had been real. "I'm fine."

She stared at his jacket and his pants. They matched the ones she wore. Why would he be wearing...?

The answer hit her like a shot put to the head. The clue had said she would find something to take with her on the race. Jace wasn't only here to give her the key.

Millie's heart dropped to her feet and kept right on going over two hundred feet to the ground below. *Splat.* "You're a contestant on *Cash Around the Globe?*"

He nodded once, his jaw tight.

She cringed, feeling duped. Used. Manipulated. Again. Just seeing Jace once made her nauseous. She couldn't imagine seeing him day after day during the race. "I can't believe you did this. You set me up."

"This wasn't my idea." Jace inserted his key and unlocked the clue box. "The producer, Pete, said there would be game twists, but I never expected to see you again."

Never wanted to see her again, Jace meant.

She felt a familiar sting.

"I didn't expect you, either." The words rushed from her mouth. Millie didn't want him to think she played a part in this. She couldn't bear him to suspect she might still harbor feelings for him. "I was hoping for a GPS unit."

"Maybe we're jumping to conclusions."

Please, oh please, let them both be wrong. "Maybe."

He opened the box. "There's only one clue pouch in there."

"So we're either in last place or…"

"Or they sent racers to different locations." He finished the thought for her.

Once she had taken his ability to complete her sentences as a sign of how close they were, how much in tune. She knew better now.

"So what does the clue say?" she asked.

Jace opened the clue pouch and pulled out a card. "Congrats on teaming together to find your second clue. Working together will be the key to your continued success in the race. The two of you are now teammates, one of eight teams competing for the cash. Using public transportation, make your way to the Marina Green to find your next clue. You don't want to come in last and go home empty-handed!"

So much for maybe.

"Teammates," she said.

A muscle twitched at his neck. He nodded. "Teammates."

Just great. Six months later, and Millie was right back

where she started. Standing in front of Jace Westfall for the world to watch and critique. She bit back a sigh. Whining or moping wouldn't change anything. Unfortunately.

"So what do we do now?" she asked.

He consulted the clue. "Find a bus."

"No, I meant..." Millie struggled for words, aware of the camera aimed at her face. She had to get over the intrusive cameras, the way she had on *The Groom,* or she wouldn't survive long. At least the network hadn't discovered a way to tap into her mind and broadcast her inner most thoughts. No, they just edited her actions and words so everyone watching assumed they knew everything about her. What she thought, how she felt, who she loved... "What do we do about...us?"

Jace's eyes were wary. "What do you want to do?"

Quit.

But she couldn't. So many children needed her to win this race. She thought about Bonnie, the petite little girl with Down syndrome who loved princesses and running the hundred yard dash, and Samuel, the gentle eight-year-old boy with Autism who was also a math wiz and javelin thrower. Each one of Millie's students was a special, precious gift. She had learned so much from them, more than she'd taught them.

"I guess—" she straightened her shoulders "—I want to win a million dollars."

It was only for thirty days, she told herself, as she climbed down the steps to the elevator. She could survive anything for a month.

Even Jace Westfall.

And then she wanted never to see him again.

What do we do about us?

Millie's earnest question sliced through Jace's pretense

of composure. He jabbed his finger at the elevator button. He only wished he knew.

Competing on *Cash Around the Globe* was supposed to save his company and his family, but now…

Jace gazed down at Millie, who rested with her eyes closed against a mural covered wall. He couldn't believe she was here, but knew he wasn't dreaming. Not with the subtle changes he couldn't have imagined.

Her trademark ponytail was longer though the ends still curled in familiar wisps. She'd lost weight though her curves were all too visible in her warm-up suit. Her eyes seemed to be a deeper green than before.

Some things hadn't changed like those damn freckles on her face that he'd always wanted to trace with his finger.

A part of him was happy to see her.

That wasn't good.

I want to win a million dollars.

He'd never expected to hear those words from sweet, adorable Millie.

What was she doing here? Her father was loaded. She didn't need the money. Not the way Jace and his family did.

The show's generous participation fee and the one million dollar prize had overcome his reluctance to step in front of the cameras and be humiliated again. But with Millie involved he was suddenly rethinking everything. Jace didn't like that. Once he made a decision he stuck with it.

Not her fault, he reminded himself.

"Do you want some water?" Jace asked.

Millie's eyelids sprang open. Wounded green eyes stared at him. "No. Thanks. I'm fine."

Yeah, right. Less than an hour into the race, Millie looked liked she'd dragged herself halfway around the globe already. Her skewed backpack was ready to topple her slender frame at any moment. She couldn't stand up straight.

This race would chew her up and spit her out. He didn't want to see her hurt again.

"I'll carry your pack," he said.

She adjusted the straps, straightening the backpack. "I've got it."

But she didn't. Not really. That put him in an awkward position.

From the first day Jace had met her, he'd felt drawn to her. She was kind and insightful and smelled like grapefruit. But the more he got to know her, the more he realized how different their lives were. How different they were. Sure, she was an incredible woman, but she wanted more from a relationship than he could give her. He'd saved them both a lot of pain by not choosing her at the end of *The Groom.*

Still he liked her and appreciated her wanting to win, but he had to be realistic. She, like his mother and sisters, was the kind of woman who needed to be coddled, cared for and protected. He didn't want to take on vulnerable Millie, too.

Maybe that's what the producers had in mind, pairing up opposites and seeing how they would get along or not. He could only imagine how this "twist" would be used once filming finished. The editing room was where hit reality television shows happened. He'd learned that lesson on *The Groom* and wasn't about to make the same mistakes again.

That was why Jace wanted—needed—a different partner.

He needed a teammate who would meet challenges head-on, never give up and do whatever it took to win the million dollar first prize. Jace couldn't afford to lose.

He stabbed the down button again. "What's taking so long?"

"It hasn't been that long," she murmured.

The elevators opened as if on cue.

He and Millie entered followed by the two camera crews. The doors closed, making it a tight fit with the backpacks and production gear, and the elevator descended.

Tension filled the static air. Darting glances, unspoken words, an uncertain future. The first two things didn't bother Jace, but the third needed to be dealt with. Now.

"You know, Freckles, the show will be challenging," he said, mindful of the cameras mere inches from them. "You can always stop if you think the race will to be too much for you."

"I can handle the race," Millie said as if she were discussing a parent-teacher conference and not a race around the world. "The clue said working together was the key to success."

Success wouldn't cut it. Jace had to win to put the money back into his struggling money management firm. His family relied on him for their paychecks and pretty much everything else. He wouldn't let them down. "I came here to win."

She raised her chin. "So did I."

"I'm not going to lose."

"Neither am I."

She still didn't get it. He had to make her understand. Hell, he needed her to quit.

"I trained for this." He'd trained as if his life depended on this race. In a way it did. If he lost, his family would pay the price. Success at all cost. That was his motto. "Trained hard."

"So did I." She met his gaze dead-on. "This pack is lighter than the one I wore when I trained."

"You wore a backpack when you trained?" he asked.

"Of course, didn't you?"

"Yes, but..." He hadn't assumed she would take this so seriously. "You said you weren't very organized."

"Let's get something straight, Jace," she said. "I didn't enter this race expecting to be teamed with someone, but I didn't enter to lose, either. I plan to give a hundred and ten percent. I expect the same from my teammate. That's you."

Seeing her determination stirred something inside Jace. He'd never thought of Millie Kincaid as competitive. Her words, full of strength and fire, surprised him. Intrigued him. Turned him on.

Maybe he'd missed that part of her during *The Groom.* Maybe he'd better just forget about that part of her altogether. He was here save to his company—and his family—from financial ruin. Period.

Jace might still be drawn to Millie, but he wasn't about to put his foot in that trap again. She expected a white picket fence future with two point three children, a dog, a cat and a minivan parked in the driveway. He wasn't the guy to give her all that. He would only end up disappointing and hurting her.

Again.

Millie pursed her pink lips, accentuating their fullness. "So what do you say?"

He'd forgotten the question, but he remembered the first time he'd kissed her. A soft, gentle kiss full of promise during a moonlit walk along the beach. He'd thought the darkness would give them a rare moment of privacy, but watching the show when it aired he realized the cameras had caught everything.

The way they were doing now.

"Jace?" her voice rose. "You can't rely only on your charm this time. Are you willing to give one hundred and ten percent?"

"Yes." He might have deserved her jab, but he sure didn't appreciate it. "As long as you're not going to be all distracted."

"Distracted?" Her forehead creased. "By what?"

Her clear green gaze made him shift uncomfortably. He was the one distracted. "By...you know. What happened before. We need to focus on the race to win."

"I'm focused." She tugged her backpack straps. "You're the one who keeps bringing up the past."

He cleared his throat. She was right. Damn it. "Let's come up with a strategy then."

"What was your strategy before?" she asked.

"Every man for himself," he admitted.

"We'll have to amend that or we won't get far." She bit her lower lip. "I have a game plan we can use."

"You?"

"Yes, me." Millie drew her brows together, and he could imagine her looking like that when she stood in front of the chalkboard to teach her students. "Too much is at stake to shoot from the hip."

The elevator stopped.

"So what's your plan?" Jace asked.

The doors opened, and the camera crews poured out.

"Run, don't walk," she explained. "And whatever we do, never look back."

Jace could handle that. "Works for me."

CHAPTER TWO

REMEMBER the game plan. All she had to do was run.

Easier said than done, Millie realized two blocks from the bus stop at the intersection of Chestnut and Fillmore Streets. Her feet pounded against the hard pavement as she tried to keep up with Jace, who ran twenty feet ahead of her.

He looked back at her. "Come on."

"Right behind you." Thank goodness the trendy Marina District was pancake flat with rows of well-kept houses, garages on the first floor, and utility cables strung from the wide, treeless streets to the rooflines. "Don't worry about me."

She could do the worrying for both of them.

Running on the track back at school was much easier than a cement sidewalk in the city, especially with garbage cans in the way, cars pulling out of driveways, a camera crew capturing every jarring step and her teammate, Jace Westfall, telling her to pick up the pace.

You can always stop if you think the race will be too much for you.

Millie inhaled sharply, the salty air filling her thirsty lungs. No doubt Jace's words had provided a perfect sound bite for the show. Had he said them for her or for the cameras or both? Not that it mattered. She couldn't stop. Not even if she wanted to. Her kids needed her to race. To win.

She pushed herself forward, focusing on Jace's back. She'd had an uninterrupted view of his butt since they both leaped off the bus, and he'd been increasing his lead with his long, powerful stride and fluid motion. Of course, any living, breathing female could appreciate how well his warm-up pants fit in all the right places.

"Be careful," he called over his shoulder. "Obstacle ahead."

What was she doing? Cute butt or not, he was simply her teammate for the duration of the race. Thinking about him in any other way would only complicate matters.

Millie focused on a thirty-something blond woman pushing a high-tech stroller toward them. "I see them."

As he maneuvered between the pair on the sidewalk and a garbage can at the curb, the woman with the baby smiled at him and flipped her hair behind her shoulder. Unbelievable. Even moms weren't immune to Jace Westfall's charms.

Millie lengthened her stride to pass the stroller and finally—finally!—caught up with him. Running next to Jace, or better yet ahead of him, would be preferable to staying behind him. The cameraman and audio guy ran alongside them. She didn't know how they kept up with all that gear.

"You're doing great, Freckles," he said, sounding not the least bit winded.

"Thanks." She snuck a peek at him. He looked totally unaffected by the running or the race or the camera focused on them. "Do you think it's much further?"

"The bus driver said if we stayed on Fillmore Street we couldn't miss the Marina Green." He glanced her way. "Why don't we stop for water?"

She pressed her lips together. Even though she'd love a sip of water, she did not need him to make allowances for her. No way would she be the weak link on their team. She was tough enough, smart enough and determined enough to handle anything *Cash Around the Globe* threw at her. Including Jace.

"I'm fine." And Millie was. She just needed to remain focused. So what if her entire world had done a one-eighty and she felt as if she'd stepped into opposite town where no meant yes and full meant empty? She could—and would—do this. "We can get a drink once we find the clue."

"If you're sure."

"I am." A sound caught her attention. "I hear a foghorn."

"We must be close. Give me your pack."

She ran faster. "I've got it."

"I don't mind."

"I do."

As the sounds of traffic grew louder, Millie accelerated. But doing so wasn't easy. She felt heavier, not from the forty pound weight strapped to her back, but from Jace's obvious lack of confidence in her abilities. She would show him.

"There's the flag," he said.

Across a multilane street on a large expanse of green grass, a familiar looking flag furled in the breeze. They'd found it. Thank goodness.

"I see it." Millie also saw two other racers, both wearing black, and her relief vanished. "There's another team."

Jace took a step off the curb. A yellow taxi zipped dangerously close. She grabbed at his backpack as he jumped back on the curb.

He didn't notice. Frustration crossed his face. "So close, yet so far."

"Close enough." Millie released the breath she hadn't realized she'd been holding. "Beating one team isn't worth risking your life for."

"Right," he agreed. "No risking death unless we see two."

Maybe she should have let him take his chances with the traffic. At least then he couldn't come back at her and say she'd held him back. "Two teams?"

"Okay, Freckles. Make that three teams."

The black team huddled over their clue. They ran to the parking lot bordering the water on the far side of the grass.

"We don't know how many teams are ahead of us," she said.

"Or behind us."

Jace's playful smile crinkled the corners of his eyes, softening the chiseled planes of his face. Tingles filled her stomach, the way they had during *The Groom,* but she knew the reaction had as much to do with his upbeat attitude as his grin. Millie felt herself being sucked into the depths of his steady gaze. And a part of her wanted to go.

Not good. Not good at all.

Millie looked into the rushing traffic to break the contact. She tapped her toe against the sidewalk eager for the light to change.

Distance. She needed distance. And a new teammate.

"Seriously," Jace said. "All we have to do is catch up to the team ahead of us and we'll be fine."

"Team?" She squinted across the lanes of speeding traffic to search for the black team and any others who had found the clue box, but saw only men playing Ultimate Frisbee and a dog walker being pulled by five dogs. "Don't you mean teams?"

"Think positive," Jace encouraged. "Isn't that what your father would say?"

Millie's insides twisted. "Uh, sure."

Her father might say those words to an audience at one of his sold-out seminars or to a reader of one of his eight bestselling self-help books, but Carl Kincaid would never say those words to his only child now that she was all grown up and a disappointment to him.

Instead her father would tell her to give up before she made a fool of herself again. He would tell her she was wasting her life teaching special needs students. He would list all the things keeping her from living up to her potential.

Millie took a deep breath. The only thing that mattered was how she saw things. Not her father. Not Jace.

Besides she'd already told herself to think positive. No big deal.

The traffic's green light changed to yellow. Jace stepped off the curb. Millie held her breath as a florist van ran the red light.

The walk sign flashed.

He grabbed her elbow. "Go, go, go."

Millie jerked her arm free and sprinted. She crossed the multilane boulevard ahead of Jace. All of her energy focused on the flag and the clue box beneath it. The scents of salt and freshly mowed grass replaced the smell of exhaust from the street behind her, but she heard the traffic pick up and allowed herself a moment's relief. The light must have changed. Any teams behind them would be stuck. Good.

Fueled by adrenaline, she beat Jace to the clue box and grabbed a pouch. Unless, she realized with a start, he let her get there first. Her spirits sagged.

"Five left," he said with satisfaction.

She tugged at the zipper to find forty dollars—a twenty, a ten and two fives—two maps, a credit card and clue. "What?"

"There are five pouches left. We're in third place."

Not last. Thank goodness.

In spite of all her training, all her pep talks to herself, Millie could hardly believe it. "Wow."

"We're doing great."

She nodded. "For now."

"Think positive," he reminded her. "What does the card say?"

She tucked a loose strand of hair behind her ear. "It's time to leave the beautiful City by the Bay so make sure you take all your belongings with you, including your heart. You will find a car parked nearby. Drive yourself to the airport (SFO) and fly to Los Angeles (LAX) where you will find a car waiting for you. To locate your next clue you'll find a car waiting for you. To locate your next clue you'll need to search among the Cherry Blossoms for the Irises and the Apples."

"Nearby?" Jace spun around. "That could mean anything."

"The black team went this way."

Millie didn't want to waste a single second. Clutching the clue pouch, she ran to the parking lot separating the Marina Green from the water. She found only random cars in every make and color imaginable.

He scanned the parking lot in the opposite direction. "That doesn't mean they knew where they were going."

"No." His lack of faith annoyed her. "But they didn't come back."

In the distance, she saw a large building with an American flag and pennant flying overhead. Closer was another building, a small square at the edge of the water surrounded by a chain link fence. And then she saw the green and blue banner. Excited, she grabbed his arm. "There!"

She didn't wait for him. She ran toward the flag and found six black Mercedes SUVs parked side by side.

"Good eyes, Freckles."

Jace opened the driver door and grabbed keys from above the visor. He removed his backpack, opened the trunk and dropped his pack inside.

"I'll take that." Jace tossed Millie's backpack into the trunk. "You've got the clue. You navigate. I'll drive."

Of course he would want to drive.

Wordlessly she climbed into the back seat. Her cameraman jumped into the passenger seat. The audio guy sat next to her. Jace's crew had said goodbye to them at Coit Tower.

He started the engine. "You buckled up?"

Millie fastened her seat belt. "Yes."

"Here we go."

As he backed out of the parking spot, she unfolded one of the maps from the clue pouch. She located the San Francisco International airport. "There are two ways to get to the airport. They look about the same distance. The difference will be the traffic we hit."

He drove past the building with the flags she'd noticed earlier. The St. Francis Yacht Club.

He turned on his blinker.

"Don't you want directions?" she asked.

The light changed. He turned left. "I know the way."

A familiar weight bore down on her. "Then why did you ask me to navigate?"

A thick bone-cutting silence descended on the car as she waited for an answer. Not that she expected one. No, Jace had only been tossing her a bone, a meaningless task to make her think she was part of this.

Too bad she hadn't let him walk into the path of that yellow cab. Tight-lipped, Millie followed their direction on the map, using the task to occupy her eyes and her hands while she controlled her heart and her voice. She had to do something. And speaking her mind with the camera rolling wouldn't do anything except make her look like a fool on national television.

Again.

The car screeched to a stop. None of the cars around them moved. Traffic looked gridlocked. Jace slapped the steering wheel. "There must be construction. Or an accident."

Millie focused on the map. "Turn right."

"Why? What do you see?"

"Right," she insisted. "Here!"

At the last second, he turned the wheel.

She breathed a sigh of relief. "Left at the next light."

She rattled off directions. A right. Another left. Straight. Jace's jaw got increasingly tight, but he followed each direction until the car nosed onto Octavia Street.

"I know where we are," he said suddenly. "This turns into US-101."

Millie held up the map. "I know."

"Great job."

She refused to show the satisfaction his words gave her. "Only doing my part for the team."

"Yeah, about that…" His words trailed off. "Look, Millie…"

A part of her wanted to avoid confrontation, the way she had during *The Groom,* but look where that had gotten her.

"Because that's what we are. A team," she emphasized

the last word. "We're supposed to work together. That's the key to success according to the clue."

He glanced in the rearview mirror. Checking for traffic? Or looking at the camera? "It's just—"

"You want to win."

"I need to win."

"So do I, Jace." She stared out the car window wondering how this was going to work or if it even could. "So do I."

Sitting in the departure area at SFO, Jace counted the money leftover after buying sandwiches for lunch and an L.A. guidebook at one of the airport shops. Good thing the camera crew paid for their own food. The money provided with each clue didn't last long. Too bad they hadn't been allowed to bring their own credit cards with them.

Announcements followed one after another, barely audible over the din of the other passengers. A stream of business people, families and flight crews rode a moving walkway to one of the many gates in the busy Terminal 3.

"I don't see any of the other teams," Millie said, sitting next to him.

Jace heard the worry in her voice and put the money into the clue pouch. He felt the need to reassure Millie. So far she'd done everything right. Keeping up with him, finding the car and navigating their trip to the airport. Her abilities surprised him. He hadn't expected her to be so decisive. So far she'd been the better teammate.

The realization made him angry. With himself.

"They're here somewhere," he said. "Don't worry."

He could do that himself.

This race meant everything, yet he wasn't thinking fast

enough. He'd made mistakes. Hell, that cab had nearly taken him out when he stepped off the curb. He wouldn't be doing his part for the team if he wound up in some hospital emergency room. Time to get his act together before they got eliminated.

"But where?" she asked.

As Millie stood, Jace watched her. After they'd purchased tickets for the flight to LAX, she'd disappeared into the bathroom for a few minutes and reappeared with her ponytail redone, her lips glossed and no windbreaker. Her T-shirt stretched across her chest. He couldn't help but appreciate the view.

Lines creased her forehead. "The black team should be at this gate."

"They might be getting lunch."

Even with her weight loss, she didn't look weak or soft. Not with her defined arm muscles and flat abs. He looked away, not wanting the camera to catch him ogling her. She was his teammate, not his plaything.

"Something's wrong." She sat, curling the edge of the clue card. "The flight boards in less than ten minutes. The black team should be here as well as whatever team was ahead of them. The next bank of LAX flights don't leave until one o'clock."

This was the woman he remembered, the quiet and cautious Millie who had won the hearts of the American television audience with her sweetness and innocence, but if she wasn't careful she would psyche herself out of the race. He couldn't afford to let that happen. At least not until he was on top of his game.

"Don't worry about the other teams," he said. "We've got our boarding passes. That's all that matters. If they don't make it to the gate on time, we'll have almost an hour and a half lead on them."

"Unless they are in the air." She tapped her foot against the carpet. "A Frontier flight departed at 10:20 and a United flight took off at 10:56."

He ran the times in his head. "No one could have gotten here that fast. The black team was only a few minutes ahead of us. Maybe they got stuck in the traffic jam or had car trouble."

"Maybe."

He gave her hand a reassuring squeeze. "Probably."

She looked down at their hands. Jace expected her to pull away from him, but she didn't so he kept his hand on hers. The bustle, the noise, everything around them seemed to fade. Touching Millie felt so...good. He didn't want to let go of her.

And then the camera guy moved.

She slipped her hand away.

Regret seeped through him. Not wanting to think about the strange emotions messing with his insides, he opened the guidebook.

"Any ideas where we should go?" Millie asked.

"Not yet."

"Well, I don't care if we have to ask every single passenger, we have to know where we are going before we land."

He stared at her in amazement.

"What?" she asked.

"You look the same. Freckles, green eyes, hair pulled back in a ponytail—"

"Same boring Millie?"

"Not boring. But not the same, either," he said. "You've changed."

"I'm the same as I've always been."

He shook his head. "There's a different intensity. A competitiveness I've never seen before."

"You just didn't look hard enough."

"Hey, I looked plenty."

But maybe not hard enough.

Not that it mattered. Choosing Desiree had been the safest choice at the time. For all of them.

Jace reached for the clue card, and Millie let him have it. "Let's figure this out so we can nap on the flight. Cherry blossoms, irises and apples."

Millie pursed her full lips. The perfect pucker for kissing. Not that he cared. Or wanted to kiss her. Much.

"What do those three things have in common?" she asked.

"They're plants." Good. He needed a task to keep from thinking about Millie. He flipped to the guidebook's index in the back. "Maybe they want us to go to a farm or nursery."

"In Los Angeles?"

"Probably not. Flowers and fruit. What about the farmer's market? That's a big tourist attraction in L.A."

Her eyes darkened. "Didn't you go there on one of your dates with Desiree?"

"Not Desiree, Charlotte."

He didn't want to talk about it. *Don't look back.* Hadn't that meant Millie wanted to leave the past behind? Still a secret part of him was flattered she remembered. That she had cared enough to keep track of what he'd done.

"Oh, yeah." Millie's eyes twinkled mischievously. "I remember Charlotte."

Jace knew exactly what Millie remembered. Charlotte was a stereotypical ditzy blonde from Kalamazoo,

Michigan, who preferred kissing to conversation because she could barely string two sentences together.

"You sent her home after that date."

"I did." Jace recalled the blonde's collagen-enhanced pout when he sent her packing. "I should have done it sooner."

"We were all surprised," Millie admitted. "She was beautiful."

"You were all beautiful."

But he'd had certain specifics he'd needed in a spouse. Charlotte had the looks, but not the brain. Desiree had the looks and brain, but not the heart. Only Millie...

Not going there. Think race. Think million dollars.

He read the travel guide. "The Farmer's Market is on the corner of Third and Fairfax."

"That's a good one." Millie reread the clue. "Do you know what we need?"

"What?"

She studied the gate area and pointed to an auburn-haired woman in her early twenties, working on a laptop. The attractive woman wore a long brown skirt with slouched boots and a turquoise blouse. Her modified bob haircut looked trendy, not dated. "Her."

"Why her?"

"She typifies *The Groom*'s target audience," Millie explained. "And chances are she's connected to the Internet."

Okay, they could use the Internet, but if the woman had watched the show, Jace didn't want another viewer telling him how stupid his bride choice had been. That's all he'd been hearing since the finale aired.

When Desiree broke up with him to pursue an acting career, the number of fans telling him via letter, e-mail and blogs he should have picked Millie increased. What people didn't realize was he knew picking Desiree had been a mistake, but picking Millie would have been worse. "I don't know, Freckles."

"Trust me on this." Anticipation filled her eyes, and he felt torn. "Please."

"Sure." He owed her this for her earlier efforts.

Millie's smile lit up her face. "Come on."

She approached the woman as if she walked up to strangers to beg a favor every day of her life. Jace's respect inched upward.

"Excuse me," she said, in a nonthreatening parent-teacher conference voice. "My name is Millie. You wouldn't happen to have a wireless connection to the Internet, do you?"

The woman glanced up from her laptop. Her mouth gaped. She snapped it closed. "Millie! Jace. I don't believe this. I never missed an episode of *The Groom*. It's my favorite show."

Yes. Target audience was dead-on. He owed Millie a hug. Scratch that, a drink.

"That's great," Millie said. "Isn't that great, Jace?"

"Fantastic. It's nice to meet you." He shook the woman's hand. "I'm Jace Westfall and this is Millie Kincaid."

"Chelsea McKenna." Her blue eyes twinkled. "I knew the thing with Desiree would never last. You two are meant to be together."

At least Chelsea hadn't called him an idiot. Jace forced a grin. "Well, we are together now."

Millie glanced at him, a warning in her eyes. "We were wondering—"

"Hey, why are we being filmed?" Chelsea peered around them to point at the film crew.

"Millie and I are on another show together."

"Wow. That's so cool." Chelsea brushed her fingers through her hair and smiled at the camera. "It's like when Amber and Rob did *The Amazing Race*. Is that the show?"

"We aren't allowed to tell you which show we're on, even if you guess the right one," Jace said.

"Oh, I understand." Chelsea looked at both of them then back at the camera like a seasoned pro. "Web sites track spoilers for reality shows. I'm sure it would cause problems if everyone knows who won before the show airs."

Millie nodded.

"Hey—" Chelsea glanced around "—how come there aren't any other contestants around?"

"That's the answer we all want to know," Millie admitted.

"Don't worry," Chelsea said. "You guys work too well together not to finish first."

Jace put his arm around Millie. He'd forgotten how she fit perfectly against him. "That's what I think, too."

She jabbed him with her elbow, but he didn't let go. Instead he held her tighter, closer. Their "target viewer" was obviously willing to help them. As long as she thought they were a couple. "We were hoping to search for some information to figure out where we should go next."

Chelsea's purple painted fingernails flew across the keyboard with lightning speed. "What do you want to search for?"

Jace read from the clue card. "Cherry blossoms, irises, apples, Los Angeles."

The woman typed the words in. "Okay, that was too easy."

"What did you find?" Millie asked from under his arm.

"An entire page with links to the Los Angeles Art

Center." She hit the return key. "Those three are paintings in the museum."

Warm satisfaction settled over Jace. Millie had come through again. He gave her a squeeze.

"Do you need directions?" Chelsea asked.

He kind of liked pretending to be a couple, but she kept pulling away from him. "We'd love directions."

"If you don't mind," Millie added.

"Mind a handsome man asking for directions?" Chelsea pulled a sheet of paper and pen from her laptop case. "How did you get so lucky, Millie?"

She took a breath. "I have no idea."

Was he the only one who heard the irony in her tone?

Chelsea wrote the directions. "Here you go."

Millie clutched the paper as if it were the Holy Grail. He didn't blame her. The directions could save them from being sent home. "Thank you so much for all your help."

"Yes, thank you, Chelsea," Jace said. "For everything."

The woman pulled out another piece of paper. "Could I have your autographs?"

Jace reluctantly let go of Millie, jotted a quick note and put his signature beneath it. "That's the least we can do, isn't that right?"

"Sure." Millie signed her name. "Here you go."

"Thanks." Chelsea's high-voltage smile could power a city for the next three days. "So when's the big date?"

He exchanged a confused glance with Millie. "You mean for the show's premiere?"

"No," Chelsea said. "I mean for your wedding."

CHAPTER THREE

WHAT was she going to do?

Millie leaned her head back against seat 12B, wedged between Jace in the aisle seat and an elderly woman by the window. Two rows ahead, Zack leaned over his seat, panning the cabin with his camera. She closed her eyes to shut him out.

Run, don't walk, she'd told Jace this morning. And *whatever we do, never look back.*

Too bad her game plan had exploded in her face. Escaping the past, not looking back, wasn't possible. Not when being with Jace meant others would recognize them and bring up *The Groom.* Bitterness coated her mouth. If only she hadn't asked Chelsea for help...

But Millie had, breaking the rules she'd set and giving the show's producers a sound bite they could use for an entire season.

I mean for your wedding.

Millie cringed. No matter how hard she raced, she couldn't run away from her past with Jace or her responsibility for what had happened.

Still no matter how awkward she felt she wasn't the same Mousy Millie who had ducked attention in high school. Nor was she the shy Millie, who kept her mouth shut during *The Groom*. She needed to talk to Jace. To apologize. She opened her eyes.

But not with the camera crew two rows ahead watching them.

Impatiently she waited for the fasten seat belt sign to illuminate on the overhead panel. Once the camera crew was strapped in, they couldn't film until the aircraft took off and reached cruising altitude.

The light flashed on, but Zack continued facing backward and filming. Ryan kept popping up.

Darn.

The plane pushed back from the gate. The flight attendant walked down the aisle pointing out the location of the oxygen masks to each row. When she saw the camera, she stopped and appeared to argue. Grumbling, Zack turned around and bobbed out of sight.

Thank goodness. Millie gripped the safety information card on her lap and leaned toward Jace.

"That was awkward back there," she whispered into Jace's ear, even though the safety talk going on and the whine of the engines while the plane taxied would make hearing her difficult. But Millie wasn't taking any chances. "I'm sorry."

"For what?"

She moistened her lips. "For approaching Chelsea."

"Are you kidding?" He sounded surprised. "She was great. You did great."

Millie wanted to believe him. "But we...I wasn't supposed to bring up the past."

"You managed to solve the clue, Freckles," Jace said, his voice warm and encouraging. "That's what matters."

"Yes, but..." Didn't he realize Chelsea's question put them in an impossible position? Millie crumpled the edge of the safety card. The engines roared, and the plane sped down the runway. "Now it sounds like we're...getting married."

As the plane lifted off the ground, he shrugged. "I never said there was a wedding date."

His warm breath against her neck sent a shiver of pleasure flowing through her. She stiffened at her body's betrayal and shoved the plane's safety brochure back into the seat pocket.

This wasn't good. "But you let her assume—"

"Chelsea believed what she wanted to believe."

"I'm not blaming you," Millie said. "This was all my fault for approaching Chelsea in the first place."

"It's not your fault, either." His deep, rich voice tried worming its way around her better judgment and common sense. "We needed help, and you got it."

His words did little to reassure her.

"Look," he continued. "Chelsea's not going to be the only person who recognizes us. And let's be honest, she liked seeing us together. That's why you knew she'd help us, remember?"

She nodded.

"She sure smiled when I put my arm around you."

"I, um, didn't notice." Millie had been too stunned to notice anything except Jace's warm, hard body pressed against her and his earthy scent surrounding her.

"Well, I did," he said. "And let's face it, having her think we're a couple is easier than trying to explain the reason we are racing together."

The plane climbed toward altitude.

"A million dollar prize is reason enough," Millie countered.

"Not for fans of *The Groom*."

"You may have a point," she conceded, remembering the bags of fan mail she received. "They do seem a bit… invested in the outcome."

"Invested? Obsessed is a better word," he said. "I received an unbelievable amount of mail, most of the letters hate mail for not picking you."

"It was your choice." A choice she was now grateful he'd made.

"Exactly, but no one seems to realize that."

"I do."

"Thank you." Gratitude filled his eyes, and she felt a little tug on her heart. "Chelsea's the first fan who's been happy to see me and that's only because you were with me."

"Seriously?"

He nodded once. "Don't forget I'm the stupid bozo."

Millie bit back a smile.

"I never thought being on *The Groom* would help us solve a clue, but it has. I say we make the most of us being together."

Her heart skipped a beat. Okay, three.

"Anything to win," he added.

The race. He meant the race. Millie forced herself to breathe. She cleared her dry throat. "Anything to win."

The aircraft leveled out. Jace peered around the seat in front of him. "We're almost at altitude. You know what that means."

"Smile for the camera."

"We need to smile and get along," he lowered his voice. "The producers want to capitalize on each team's conflicts. Intense personal dramas played out during the race will translate into ratings. The less we fight, the less camera time we'll have."

"The less time the better." She smiled. "So no conflict."

"No conflict." Jace smiled back.

Her heart fluttered.

Uh-oh. Millie swallowed. The real conflict might actually be between her head and her heart.

No conflict seemed to be working. The cameraman, Zack, and sound guy, Ryan, kept sending each other frustrated looks, but Jace couldn't be happier. The plane arrived on time, a car was waiting for them and the directions to the Los Angeles Art Center were spot-on. Most importantly, he and Millie were making this fledgling partnership work. He only hoped the other teams were providing the necessary amounts of juicy drama so they would be left alone.

"Here's some money." She passed him dollar bills over his shoulder. "For parking."

He paid the fee and parked. "Let's grab the packs."

"I don't think we should take the packs," Millie said, sounding hesitant.

Jace slammed his door. "Why not?"

She moistened her lips. "Art museums usually have rules about bringing large bags and stuff inside."

Instinct told him to bring the packs, but he only went to museums to attend social events. Backpacks weren't acceptable accessories at soirees like those so he had no idea if she was correct or not.

"At least every art museum I've been to," Millie added.

The clock was ticking. Every second they stood here kept them from finding the next clue. Jace surveyed the parking garage, but saw no one. No other teams, no tourists to tell him whether to take the packs or not.

"We might not have to come back to the car," he said.

"Would you rather have to turn around at the entrance?"

Millie had a point. But what if they were told to take public transportation or a taxi or a million other possibilities from the museum? How much time would a trip back to the car add? Enough time to be eliminated?

No, Jace didn't want to think about that. He just had to make a decision.

She bit her lip.

No conflict, he remembered and locked the car. "Let's leave the packs."

Zack held the camera steady, but didn't hide his frown. The cameraman had wanted a fight, anything to up the tension that had disappeared since the flight.

Jace grinned. Getting along with Millie was going to drive the production crew crazy. That in itself would be worth losing a finishing spot or two on this leg of the race.

Of course, if the decision to leave the backpacks in the car turned out to be wrong…

Millie ran to the elevator, and Jace followed. As soon as the doors opened, Jace exited. Millie was right at his heels. Rows of cherry blossom trees stood like sentries, standing watch over the entrance pavilion.

Millie stared at the trees and beyond them the neo-Gothic buildings with shooting fountains. "This is incredible."

"No kidding." But they weren't here to admire the grounds or architecture.

"I'd love to bring my students."

Students? Jace couldn't believe she was thinking about them at a time like this. "We need to focus."

Wide-eyed, she stared at a large statue. "I'm focused."

But on the race? That was the question.

At the entrance, Jace paid their admission and grabbed

two maps. As he handed one to Millie, his fingers brushed her skin. So soft, so smooth. His hand lingered until the sound of shouting made him realize what he was doing.

Two tall, athletic guys in matching green warm-up pants and T-shirts yelled at a female attendant stationed at another entry kiosk about keeping their backpacks with them. A camera crew filmed them. The attendant remained calm, never raising her voice, but Jace observed a scowling security guard running over.

Jace glanced at Millie, who studied the map, not distracted by the yelling or tourists passing by.

"Good call on the packs, Freckles."

"Thanks." She waved her map. "I know where to go."

No, "I told you so." No demand for compliments or gratitude. At least that much about her hadn't changed. Man, she was sweet.

"The pictures are exhibited in the Pacific Building," she said. "On the same floor. The clue box has to be there."

Jace jerked his mind back to the race. He was the one having trouble focusing now.

"We need to beat the green team," he said. "Keep your eyes open for flags. You never know—"

"What the other teams might pull," she finished for him.

She sprinted ahead, zigzagging around tourists as she climbed the grand stairway leading to the museum. He followed her through the courtyard. Two racers, dressed in identical black warm-up suits, skidded to a stop.

"Hey, blue team. The clue's not here," one of them, a blond surfer type, yelled. "We're at the wrong place."

"Yeah, we searched everywhere." The dark haired guy gave Millie the once-over. "I'm Matt. This is Derek."

The blond guy nodded.

Jace noticed a clue card sticking out of his pocket. No doubt the two men were trying to throw them off. The best thing to do was get away from them. Now. "Let's—"

"I'm Millie." She gazed shyly up at them through her eyelashes. "It's nice to meet you both."

"You, too," Matt said, never once taking his eyes off her. "We wouldn't want you guys to waste time around here."

Yeah, right. So why don't you just tell us where you found your clue? Jace wanted to punch the guy. Not only for misleading them, but for leering at Millie.

"That's so nice of you." She stared up at him as if Matt were the most interesting man she'd ever met. "Isn't it, Jace?"

Millie needed to wise up to the world. And men. Those two guys on the black team were nothing but players. And if she weren't careful, she'd be their next mark. Jace motioned to the clue sticking out of the pocket. A subtle nod of her head told him she'd seen it.

Matt chuckled. "We're nice guys, Millie."

"Very nice," Derek added. "Matt here is a paramedic if you need rescuing. I'm a physical therapist if you have anything that hurts."

"Thanks," she said.

"Anytime." Matt cocked a brow. "And I mean that."

Jace wanted to throw up.

"Since you're such nice guys, I'd hate for you to forget to check the gardens," she said. "Cherry blossoms, apples and irises are plants."

"Millie," Jace said, harsher than he'd intended.

"The gardens." Matt winked at her. "Thanks for the tip."

"Anytime," she said. "And I mean that, too."

She'd seen they had the clue. What was she doing?

"See ya, Millie," Derek said. "Bye Millie's dude."

The two men headed toward the garden.

Jace grabbed hold of her hand. "Come on."

As soon as the other team was out of sight, he let go of her. "What was that all about?"

"Playing dumb so they underestimate us," she explained. "Do you think they bought it?"

"Yes." He sure had. "I nominate you team captain."

"Good, because I know what we need to do."

"What's that?" he asked.

Her green eyes twinkled. "Find some apples and irises."

"I'm right with you."

And Jace meant it. He couldn't have asked for a more intelligent, worthy teammate than Millie Kincaid.

"I hope we made the right choice," Millie said on their way to the "Solo Stoppage," a challenge from the clue they'd picked up between the paintings at the museum. Each teammate had to successfully complete their separate tasks to win the next clue.

"We did." He sounded so confident. "Whatever it is, you can do it."

His words didn't reassure her.

When they were told to choose between restyle or restore before reading the clue, she'd thought the restyle task would be decorating. Millie loved watching decorating shows on television and could easily handle a task like that, but now she had no idea what was in store for either of them.

She reread the clue card. "Drive yourself to the Sunset Towers Hotel on Sunset Boulevard where stars of the silver screen such as Errol Flynn, Marilyn Monroe and John Wayne once lived. Follow the flags to where one of you will be restyled and the other restored."

Insecurity grabbed hold of her like an old friend.

Millie didn't want to make a mistake and be the reason they got eliminated. Jace watched her through the rearview mirror. "What?" she asked.

"Just remember—"

"Think positive."

He nodded.

Jace parked the car in front of an Art Deco building that looked like something out of an old movie. He jumped out of the car and opened the trunk. "We're taking our packs with us."

She wasn't about to argue and put on her pack. "I see a flag."

The flag was positioned outside a door along Sunset Boulevard. One step inside the elegant salon with high ceilings and a wall of windows, Millie froze. Her stomach did a half gainer with a twist. Forget interior decorating. A place like this was about redoing a person, not a room.

She glanced around the elegant waiting area with a couch, two chairs and a coffee table with an elaborate, colorful floral arrangement. The mauve and purple decor was probably intended to soothe clients, as was the jazzy music playing, but she only felt out of place. Completely.

At least the clue about her being restyled made sense. Still that didn't quell her uncertainty or diminish her unease.

What exactly were they going to do to her?

Jace bumped into her backpack, pushing her further into the salon. "Sorry."

"Welcome." A beautiful woman with flawless makeup and hair greeted them. An additional camera crew was there. "Which one of you is restore and which is restyle."

He stepped forward. "I'm restore."

"Oh, we have something special for you." She hit a button. "If you'll have a seat, an attendant will be right with you."

Jace removed his backpack and sat on the sofa. He didn't act or look out of place. Of course, Millie realized, he wouldn't. He probably had his hair cut at a trendy salon like this. "Good luck, Freckles."

Too nervous to talk, she gave him the thumbs-up.

The woman walked around the front desk to Millie. "Come with me, please."

Millie followed her into the actual salon. Zack and Ryan went with her. One of the guys from the black team, Derek, was getting his hair washed by an exotic looking woman with amazing highlights while a cameraman filmed him. He didn't seem to notice her. Or maybe he was ignoring her. After all, he and his teammate had tried to pull a fast one on her and Jace.

At least they'd beat the green team here and weren't in last place. A rush of pride made Millie straighten.

"Please put on a brown smock." The receptionist motioned to a door. "Then you can get started."

This was a task, part of the race, and Millie should be hurrying, but she couldn't reach for the door handle. Not when she had no idea what would happen to her when she walked out. She couldn't stop thinking about that one episode of *Amazing Race* when they shaved a female contestant's head.

"What are they going to be doing to me?" she asked. "Wash hair and blow dry? Makeup? Manicure?"

Make me bald?

She didn't put a lot of effort into how she looked, but the idea of no more hair made her stomach clench.

"Our amazingly talented stylists are going to give you

a whole new look. Hair, eyebrows, makeup. The works minus hair color. There's not enough time for that," the receptionist explained. "Still, you'll walk out of here looking and feeling like a new you."

"Oh, boy." Good. Millie got to keep her hair. Well, maybe not all of it. She wondered how Jace was being restored and hoped he was okay.

"Just wait." The woman smiled. "You'll love it."

Conscious of the camera on her, Millie smiled back. But at least it didn't sound like she was going to lose her hair or walk out a blond or redhead or rainbow colored.

"We serve Malibu Family Wines," the receptionist said. "Would you like a glass?"

"Please," Millie said. Though the way her insides were shaking so much one glass might not be enough.

"I'll bring some chocolates and cookies, too."

"Great."

Only it wasn't. Millie stepped into the dressing room. The last time she'd had a makeover, albeit a mini one, disaster and embarrassment had struck.

What would happen this time?

She wasn't sure she wanted to find out.

Jace joined Matt from the black team on the outside terrace. The cushioned chaise lounges were the perfect seats to relax after the most amazing massage ever experienced.

"So you found the clue at the museum," Matt said, looking as lazy as Jace felt.

"We did." No thanks to him and his teammate "dude," but Jace wasn't about to air dirty laundry in front of Matt's cameraman. Being a good sport was important. "You guys must have found your clue right after we did."

Matt sipped his glass of ice water instead of answering.

Good. Jace didn't want to think about the race. The only thing he wanted to do was sleep. He'd never felt so relaxed in his life. All tension had evaporated thanks to their "restore" task—a hot stone massage. Not a sliver of stress remained after heated river rocks were placed on him while the massage therapists—two of them—worked magic with their talented hands. Jace didn't think he was going to be able to drive.

"How are you and your little costar getting along?" Matt asked.

Some of the tension that had been rubbed out of Jace returned. "Why do you ask?"

"I didn't know I was racing with Derek. The loser stole my girl. The green team had no idea they'd be together so I'm assuming you and Millie were thrown together, too."

"Yes," Jace admitted. "But it's working out fine."

"She's mighty fine," Matt said. "I haven't met many women who I'd say this about, but she's perfect wife material. Why didn't you pick her on *The Groom?*"

Jace deliberately closed his eyes. He wasn't about to get into that discussion with one of his competitors. On camera. Millie would be a great wife for the right guy. Just not him.

Or Matt.

The guy whistled. Jace ignored him.

"Whoa," Matt said. "I mean. Wow."

"I'm finished," Millie said quietly. She sounded shy and vulnerable, and Jace hoped she did well on her task. Not just for the race's sake, either. "We can get our clue."

He opened his eyes. The most beautiful woman he'd ever seen stood at the entrance to the terrace.

"Mill—" He fell off the chaise, hitting the tiled floor with a thud.

She ran to him. "Are you okay?"

No. His tongue felt thick. So did his head. This couldn't be Millie. Where was her trademark ponytail with curly strands sticking out? What was covering up her freckles? Not that she had the stuffed caked on her face. She looked natural, with just enough makeup to highlight her best features. But…

She reached her arm out. "Let me help you up."

All he could do was stare. Her shorter shoulder length hair fell in soft layers framing her face. Her eyes seemed greener, her lips fuller.

Yet he saw the Millie he knew in the tentative expression on her face. In the way she held her hand out waiting for him to meet her halfway. And that somehow made things…worse.

Perfect wife material? Most definitely.

Why didn't you pick her? Jace had no idea.

CHAPTER FOUR

AS MILLIE pulled Jace to his feet, she struggled not to jerk her hand from his. The way he stared made her feel exposed, vulnerable, naked. But she couldn't tell whether he liked the way she looked or not. Millie wanted to know. Badly.

She released his hand. "Are you okay?"

"I'm fine." His gaze remained locked on hers, and she swallowed around the blow-dryer-size lump in her throat. "The hot stone massage left me feeling like a piece of overcooked pasta."

"At least you're destressed." Something Millie wished she could say about herself. She waited for him to say something about her new look. The way he kept looking at her had to be a good sign. Right? "Or rather, restored."

He nodded.

Hmmm. Maybe Millie needed to be more direct. Not that she was fishing for a compliment. Okay, she admitted. Maybe she was. "So what do you think?"

"We should get the clue."

Millie wanted to scream. She didn't want the clue. She wanted his opinion. Now. She'd never considered herself to be the foot-stomping, pouty type, but if anyone could drive her to such actions Jace Westfall could.

She didn't get him.

That wasn't a new development, she realized with a pang of regret. So why was she disappointed? Derek had called her "hot." Matt had whistled when he first saw her. Who cared what Jace thought? Except...

He acted as if she was still the same old Mousy Millie, not Magnificently Sexy Millie as her hair designer had deemed her. And though she didn't feel magnificently sexy, she sure didn't feel the least bit mousy.

She felt like she could take on the world.

Or at least she had until Jace's nonreaction.

"What's the holdup?" he asked.

She glanced at Matt, who was practically panting at her. That reaction would have to do. She flipped her hair behind her shoulder, the way she'd seen the other contestants on *The Groom* do. Obviously Jace was immune to whatever magic the stylists had worked on her. She wasn't going to allow him to ruin this moment for her.

Millie pursed her lips. She didn't need his approval or his compliments. She didn't want them.

"Nothing's holding me up," she said finally.

"Then let's go. We may have the lead."

Millie nodded. "The green team's here, too. One of them was having his hair washed when I finished."

Jace placed his hand on the small of her back, and she nearly gasped from the unexpected contact. "Let's get the clue and grab our packs."

As they hurried to the front desk, he kept his hand on her. His touch was light, but seemed to burn through the waistband of her pants. She ignored the heat emanating from the spot.

It didn't mean anything, Millie rationalized.

She'd once found him attractive during *The Groom*.
She'd even kissed him, but who cared? A trace of the chem-
istry, some half-life of attraction, still existed.

That was all.

As the receptionist handed him a clue, Jace moved his
hand off Millie.

Good, she thought. Except now she felt a little...cold.
Which meant Millie was losing it. Big time.

Reality show equaled make-believe. She couldn't lose
herself in that fantasy again. "What does the clue say?"

"Drive to LAX. Fly to La Aurora International Airport.
Once there, take a taxi to the National Palace of Culture
where you will find your next clue. You will have one
hundred dollars for the next leg of this race."

They grabbed their packs.

Outside the salon, the sun hung low in the golden red and
pink sky. They ran toward their car with Zack and Ryan.

"La Aurora International Airport," Millie repeated.
"Where is that?"

"Mexico? Central or South America?" He put on his
backpack. "We can find out when we get to the airport."

The threat of being the first ones sent home lingered
like the smog hovering over Los Angeles. "I don't like
not knowing."

He studied her for a moment. "Me, either. But we're
doing great, Freckles. We could be in first place."

She nodded, wanting to believe him.

"We'll figure out where to go." He opened the trunk and
tossed her backpack inside. "Don't worry."

"How did you know I was worrying?" she asked.

Jace dropped his pack in. "You tug on a piece of hair."

"I..." Millie wanted to disagree until she realized she

was holding onto several strands of hair. She let go of them as if she were holding dynamite. "How did you figure that out?"

"When we rode the glass elevator to the top of that restaurant in the downtown skyscraper on our second date."

The candlelit dinner with a strolling violin player rushed back. A chocolate soufflé served with two spoons. Everything had been orchestrated so perfectly by the show with the exception of the restaurant location. "Heights aren't my favorite thing."

"You could have told me that."

"You didn't pick the restaurant."

"No, I didn't." He handed her the car keys. "You drive."

She stared at the keys on her open palm. "Me?"

"The massage left me too relaxed," he said. "I don't think I should drive. Is that going to be a problem?"

"N-no problem." So what if she was used to driving in Two Rivers, Oregon, a small town with two stoplights, a McDonald's, corner market, café and feed store? It wasn't as if he'd asked her to climb a mountain or jump from an airplane. Millie curled her fingers around the keys, the metal digging into her skin. "I drive every day."

At the airport, Jace kept looking at Millie. He couldn't take his eyes off her. She looked so different. So good. But it wasn't just the makeover. She seemed more excited and happy than before. Hell, she practically sparkled.

"Any sign of the pink team?" Millie asked, looking up from a map of Guatemala City.

Damn, she'd caught him staring at her. Again.

Maybe she hadn't noticed. And maybe UFOs were going to land at Disneyland tonight.

"No."

"I hope they're okay."

That was so like Millie. To worry about two strangers who were competing against her for a million dollars.

Zack moved closer with the camera. Jace clenched his jaw. No doubt the camera had caught him staring at Millie.

"Don't worry, Freckles," he said. "They have a camera crew with them. They'll be fine."

With the late night flights to Guatemala City leaving within a couple of hours of each other, no team would have a large lead to fall back on. That's why Jace held their boarding passes for the flight departing at eleven o'clock as if they were golden tickets.

In a way, they were.

Thanks to Millie's driving and his navigating, they'd arrived first at the airport. Who would have thought she could pass cars like a NASCAR driver at Daytona? He smiled, thinking about her wearing a one-piece driver suit. She'd look sexy.

Sexy. The word seemed incongruous to the Millie he'd known during *The Groom,* yet now the word fit her.

Jace shifted in his seat.

She looked around. "Everyone else is here."

"Yes." Two teams, blue and black, had seats on the eleven o'clock departure. The green and purple teams had seats on the eleven forty-five flight. Yellow, orange and red team had seats on the eleven fifty-five flight. "That doesn't mean anything."

"It does if the pink team is already gone."

"They probably just got lost," Jace said. "Remember, we don't care who's behind us."

"Then let's figure out where we need to go once we arrive."

As she leaned toward him, the strong citrus scent of her new shampoo surrounded him. He caught himself wanting another sniff.

Enough was enough. He was here to win a race, not find a girlfriend. Jace backed away from her.

"It's okay," Millie said.

"Okay?"

"My restyle." Staring at the map, she ran her finger along a crease on the paper. "The hair and makeup might have changed, but I'm still the same person inside."

"I know," Jace mumbled. "That's the problem."

"Problem?" she asked. "It's not a problem that you don't like this new look of mine."

"You think I don't like it?"

"You don't."

His gaze raked over her. The blush to Millie's cheeks only made her more attractive. He wanted to take her in his arms and show her what he thought of her new look. But he couldn't. Not with the camera filming them. Not if he wanted to win this race.

"I like it," he said finally.

"But…"

"But what?" He hated the uncertainty in her voice and eyes. "You look—" beautiful, gorgeous, perfect "—great."

"Thanks. I feel…great." The corners of her mouth curved upward. "And I think we have a shot at the million."

The camera continued to film them. No matter where they were, Zack and Ryan were right there next to them, too.

He stared at her. Attracted not only by what he saw, but what he heard, too. "You're right."

Her grin reached her eyes. "Of course, I'm right."

Her increased confidence shot through like an arrow

piercing his heart. What was going on? Being attracted to
his teammate wasn't a good idea. It had to stop. Now.

The landing gear hit the runway. The jolt woke Millie.
She opened her eyes and found herself staring at Jace.
His chest to be exact. Her head rested against his arm
and her hand on his...thigh. She jerked her arm away and
sat straight.

She waited for him to say something, to laugh, but she
heard nothing. A sideways glance told her Jace was asleep.

Thank goodness. She'd avoided that embarrassment.

Still this was not how she wanted to start the second day
of the race. She caught sight of the red recording light and
noticed Zack's camera focused on her.

Oh, no. First, the wedding talk. Now, her using Jace as
a pillow. What was going to go wrong next?

As if on cue, Jace, his eyes still closed, turned toward her.
He nuzzled his head against her neck. "You smell so good."

The air *whooshed* from her lungs.

He was still asleep. He didn't know what he was saying,
but the words made her feel warm and tingly inside.

Not good.

She jabbed him with her elbow.

"Wha—"

"Good morning." With a forced smile on her face, Millie
motioned to the camera with her head. She wasn't sure
anymore how she felt or what she wanted or what she
wanted to do about it. But she sure wasn't going to have
that decision made for her in the cutting room and dis-
cussed over office watercoolers for the next six months.
"Welcome to Guatemala."

"We're here already." He glanced around, looking half-asleep and dazed and totally adorable. "I feel like I just closed my eyes."

She fought the urge to ruffle his hair and tell him to go back to sleep. That would be a bad move on camera. Teammates didn't ruffle each other's hair.

"Well, there's no time to sleep now." She tried mustering some semblance of enthusiasm. Not easy with the film rolling. "Not until we reach the check-in point."

"That has to be sometime soon."

"I hope so." Guatemala City was their third city and second country in less than twenty-four hours. Somehow she'd managed to survive being attached at the hip to Jace. Not literally, but that's what it felt like. "Otherwise, they might have to retitle the show *Crash Around the Globe*."

Jace laughed. The rich, warm sound surrounded her. She wet her lips.

Hungry, she rationalized. She must be hungry for breakfast.

Outside the terminal, Millie flagged down a white taxi, and Jared negotiated a price with the driver since the cab had no meter. She noticed how they each had used their own strengths to find transportation.

At the Palace of Culture, the next clue sent them on a quest. They ran through hallways decorated with wood-carvings and artwork looking for the *espacio de trono*. They kept seeing glimpses of other teams—purple, yellow and green.

"We can't lose any more time," Jace said. "The teams are too packed together."

"Let me find help." Millie asked a tourist who spoke English to translate the clue. "The throne room is where we'll find the next clue."

Jace checked a map and ran to the room where he found a clue pouch. "We're getting this teamwork down."

She felt a tingling sensation in her stomach, but that had more to do with her increased confidence and working well with Jace than anything else. Two heads were better than one. "Yes, we are."

He handed her the clue card. "You can read it."

"Take a bus to the market at Chichicastenango. Find the stand selling fabric with this pattern." She held up the colorful striped pattern against a bright orange background attached to the card. "Once you find the fabric, you will be given your next clue. A warning—the market only operates on Thursday and Sunday so if you don't arrive before closing time, you'll have a long wait."

As her stomach knotted, Millie realized she was pulling on her hair. She held onto the clue card with both hands.

Jace glanced at his watch. "It's early. We'll make it."

She appreciated his reassurance and his confidence. He was right. They could do this. "Let's find the bus."

Outside, Millie took a deep breath. Acclimating to the almost five thousand foot altitude and equally high humidity wasn't going to be easy. She raised her hair off the back of her sweaty neck. "Which way should we go?"

"The fastest way."

"Okay." She looked around the crowded street. "Let's find someone who can help us."

An American student, participating in a language immersion class, recognized them from *The Groom*. Millie couldn't believe how being on that show might help them win the million dollars. The student escorted them to a bus stop, suggesting they take a tourist bus not a chicken bus.

"A chicken bus probably won't be as bad as a cattle car." Millie tried thinking positively even though the thought of the cheaper transportation mode was less than appealing. Could there really·be chickens on board? "It will save us money, too."

"True," Jace said. "But are you up for a three and a half hour ride on something called a Chicken Bus?"

"I was trying to think positively."

"Good for you, but anything with the word chicken that has wheels demands realistic thinking."

"So you want to spend the extra money?" she asked.

"Yes."

Relief seeped through her. "Okay."

"But way to go on the positive thinking."

His compliment made her stand taller. Until she saw all the children wearing bright colored clothing playing on the sidewalk. Some were barefoot. Millie sucked in a breath.

"What's wrong, Freckles?" Jace asked.

"Those kids." She rubbed her watery eyes. "They are the same age as my students, but these kids have so little compared to the ones at my school."

The children laughed and ran around the corner. A lone rail-thin boy kicked a faded, peeling, deflated soccer ball.

"It looks like his ball got run over," Jace said.

"He needs a new one."

"And some food." He reached into his pocket and handed her money. "Why don't you give him this?"

She stared at the money in her hand. Not much but more—a lot more—than she would have expected from him. Jace's generosity tugged at her heart.

A quiet thanks was all she could manage. Emotion

clogged her throat. Once again Jace had surprised her only this time in a good way. She couldn't help but wonder what he would do next.

And if she'd be ready for it.

On the road to Chichicastenango, Jace closed his eyes. He hadn't slept much on the flight. How could he rest with Millie sleeping against him? Her soft, warm breath brushing his arm like a kiss? The exotic scent of her shampoo surrounding him like ambrosia?

Hell, he could smell her now.

He opened his eyes. No way was he going to sleep.

The crowded bus hit a rut on the road. Sitting on the aisle, Millie grabbed onto the seat in front of her. "I think my spleen and liver may have changed places."

"Ouch," Jace said, noting the pained expression on her face.

Zack and Ryan smiled. The camera crew might not be seeing the conflict they wanted, but they were getting some good shots and sound bites between being bounced around themselves.

Good thing they hadn't taken the chicken bus.

The tourist bus hit another hole. Millie flew up off the set. He grabbed her, his hands circling her thin waist and pulling her down. "Where do you think you're going?"

She moistened her lip. "I—I don't know."

That made two of them.

Time seemed to stop. Her warmth seeped through her T-shirt and his palms grew hot. He didn't want to let go of her.

A dog barked behind them. A baby cried in front of them.

He should let her go. But they might hit another pothole. If he thought hard enough he could probably come up with a couple more reasons to keep touching her. Which gave him a good reason to remove his hands.

Millie scooted away from him. Well, as far as the bus seat allowed her to go and remain seated. She glanced back at the family sitting behind them. The children sang a song.

The faraway look in her eyes intrigued Jace. "Do they remind you of your students?"

"Yes." Her lips curved in a soft smile. "It's hard not to think about them since they're the reason I'm here."

"What do you mean?" he asked.

"Whatever money I win goes to my school. With all the budget problems, programs are being cut, and that hurts all the students. Not just special needs kids."

"I had no idea you were doing this for your school." Okay, now things were making sense. Millie had told him her dad wanted her to work for him, not teach at a public school. No wonder she needed the money, but still to go through all this for a bunch of kids who probably don't want to be in school anyway. "That's generous of you."

"Not really," she said humbly. "I'm sure we all have our reasons for wanting the money."

He thought about his own reasons.

"Jace?"

He didn't want to tell her and the cameras his firm was failing, that without the prize money he might lose everything. "An influx of capital would take my business to the next level."

"Your family works with you, right?"

For me. "Yes, they do."

"So you're racing for them. Your family."

Nodding, he stared at the ground. He couldn't have

answered even if he tried. Not just his awareness of the cameras, but his surprise at how Millie had figured it out.

"That shows how much you love them, Jace," Millie said, her voice full of compassion.

He raised his gaze until it met hers.

"They must be so proud of you," she continued.

He thought of his mother and his two sisters. "They will be if I win."

"Oh, sure." Millie laughed. "Only if you win."

Jace wasn't joking. His family needed him to come through for them. He hadn't ever let them down. He wouldn't this time. "If you knew them, you'd understand."

"I'm sorry I never met them," she said softly.

He was suddenly sorry, too.

"I have their picture," he volunteered.

Her expressive eyes widened. "You brought your family's picture on the race?"

He nodded. "My memento."

"That's sweet."

He was embarrassed. Pleased. "What memento did you bring?"

Millie glanced back at the kids in the back. "A report card the kids made me during teacher appreciation week. They graded me in different subject areas."

"Did you get straight A's?" he asked.

"No." She chuckled. "I got a lot of F's."

He raised a brow. "You?"

"They used their own grading system."

The look in her eyes softened, and took Jace back to their last date, to a hotel suite in Whistler. He and Millie had spent the day cozying in front of the fireplace with mugs of hot chocolate and a plate of freshly baked cookies while a blizzard raged outside. They'd talked about her family and his. About what they wanted out of life. That was the most relaxing time he'd ever spent, but he'd also seen their differences.

Millie was a quiet, easygoing teacher who liked small town living, had carved a life out for herself there and wanted to have a family of her own. Jace, on the other hand, was still trying to build his life in the city. He wasn't sure whether he wanted kids or not. He just wanted to make things better for his family and was driven to succeed.

Their lives were so different he couldn't see how they would fit together. He hadn't wanted to deal with the likely consequences of trying, with Millie or himself getting their hearts bruised.

So he'd chosen Desiree.

Jace took a sharp breath. Millie's questioning gaze met his.

"What did F stand for?" he asked.

"F for fun." Her face lit up, the way it always did when she talked about her students. She was so beautiful, even with smudges of dirt on her cheeks and circles under eyes. "Of course, it took me a few minutes to figure that out."

He laughed. "That must have been a long few minutes."

"You have no idea."

Oh, he might have a clue. Every minute he spent with her he felt his attraction growing and his resolve weakening. And unfortunately, no end was in sight.

The end was in sight.

For today, at least.

Millie saw the flag. Colt, the host of the show, stood on a mat signifying the checkpoint for this leg of the race.

Relief flowed through her tired body. A long, hot afternoon searching the numerous stalls of the market for the exact pattern match of their swatch had her running on fumes. She'd rummaged through so many colorful fabrics her hands ached. She could still hear the fireworks exploding from homemade rockets, the smell mixing with the scents of the market foods and incense being burned nearby on the steps of an old church. They'd made their way to Panajachel, where they scoured the town, on the shore of the gorgeous Lake Atitlan, for their final clue for this leg of the race.

"Run," Jace said, lengthening his stride.

Her entire body hurt. She felt lightheaded. She needed water and to hibernate for the rest of the summer. "I can't."

"One hundred percent," he reminded her. "You've done it all day long. You can do it now."

Jace was right. She could do this.

Not for him. Not for her. But the kids.

Millie dug deep—past the dirt, the hunger, the exhaustion—for an extra boost of energy. Using all her willpower, she picked up her pace and passed him.

He quickly caught up with her. "Told you so."

His voice told her he was smiling. "Yes, you did."

"There."

The flag fluttered in the hot breeze. She could taste dirt from the trail, but it didn't matter. The checkpoint was only a hundred feet away.

She had made it.

She and Jace had both made it.

Heart pounding, feet thudding, she looked at a picture of the globe on the green and blue mat. Yellow stars marked the cities they'd visited. Red lines marked the path they'd traveled.

Millie pounced on the mat, jumping with both feet like her students did playing hopscotch at recess. Sweat dampened the hair around her face. Her leg muscles ached from the workout. Her stomach tingled with anticipation.

"Millie and Jace," Colt said with a deadpan expression.

They weren't last. She just knew they couldn't be the last team to arrive at the layover.

"You are team number three."

The rush of relief overshadowed the wave of excitement. Tension evaporated from her body. Tears welled in her eyes.

Jace picked her up off the ground and hugged her. Tight. "We did it, Freckles."

"We did."

His strong arms pulled her closer against his hard body. Her feet dangled in the air. He was hot. Sweaty. Just like her.

And she'd never felt better in her entire life.

Millie felt his heart beat against her chest. She stared up at him, her mouth mere inches away from his. A kiss. She wanted him to kiss him. On the lips.

But wait… She and Jace weren't alone. Colt, Zack, Ryan and the camera were here, too. Panic shot through her.

Okay, Jace was only giving her a hug. So what if he had held her tight and her feet hadn't touched the ground for sixty seconds? The hug had nothing to do with physical attraction and everything to do with appreciation for a job well done.

Not desire.

Not delight.

Simple relief they had made it this far. Together.

Her and Jace.

The fact she'd wanted him to kiss her had absolutely nothing to do with anything, either. Too much exertion explained that irrational thought. They'd been racing for so long without a real meal or enough water or a decent night's sleep to think straight.

"So what do you think about having a teammate for the remainder of the race, Jace?" Colt asked.

Jace placed her on the ground, but still looked at her.

Millie's heart rate increased. She knew he hadn't thought she'd bring much to the team when they'd met up at Coit Tower, but she'd proven herself since then. Kept up, too. Surely he'd had a change of heart or he wouldn't have been so encouraging during that final push before the check-in point.

"It's worked out so far," he said finally.

"What about you, Millie?" Colt asked.

Clearing her dry throat, she thought of various sound bites the show was probably wanting. "We work well together."

That was all they were going to get from her today.

"Great." Colt smiled. "Enjoy your layover. There are showers, food and cots."

"A shower would be good," Jace said, resting his arm around Millie's shoulder.

Not trusting her voice, she nodded.

A shower would be good. The bathroom was the one place Jace and the camera couldn't follow her.

CHAPTER FIVE

ELEVEN and a half hours later, rays of sunlight peeked through the horizon. Not used to being up this early, Millie stood in the bathroom and splashed cold water on her face.

She felt better physically. She'd filled her stomach with delicious food from an overflowing buffet of local dishes, washed the dirt and sweat away in a not-so-hot shower and slept ten hours on a more-comfortable-than-it-looked cot in a one-room lodge on Lake Atitlan, but emotionally she was a wreck.

Not about the race itself, but being with Jace.

Reliving what happened during *The Groom* was one thing, but this unexpected—unwanted—attraction to him was another.

Millie shivered, knowing her reaction had nothing to do with the cool morning air and high elevation.

She didn't blame Jace for rejecting her in the past. They didn't want the same things out of life. His choosing Desiree had been for the best. And boy, was she glad to have missed out on the media circus that would have followed their engagement and wedding.

But she blamed herself for falling for him all over again.

Thinking about him. Watching him fall asleep. Wanting him to kiss her.

Millie grimaced.

She was allowing herself to be swept up in a fantasy also known as reality television. The locations they visited might be real, but nothing else was. Not her feelings. Not even Jace.

Sure he felt real, not only his strong arms and solid body, but his encouragement, confidence and humor. Yet the real Jace Westfall was a driven image-conscious competitor. Millie couldn't allow herself to forget he would do anything it took to win.

Even, her insecurities whispered, sweet-talk a woman he once rejected into racing to win.

Well, Millie straightened, she didn't need his encouragement to want to win. She didn't need him.

With her resolve firmly in place, Millie dried her face and rubbed on a moisturizer. The last thing she wanted to put on was makeup, but she'd promised the makeup expert at the salon she'd at least attempt to replicate his magic during the race. Thank goodness he'd supplied her with an overflowing travel bag since she usually only wore sunscreen and a fruity-tasting lip gloss.

An older woman in an orange T-shirt and warm-up pants entered the rest room. "Good morning."

Millie pulled out the round container of mineral powder foundation and a stubby round brush and tried to remember how to apply it. "Hi."

"You're the one from *The Groom*."

Millie wondered if she'd forever be identified by a six-week reality television experience. No one seemed to care she'd lived twenty-six years before and continued to have a life now.

Still she nodded. "I'm Millie."

"Constance Sutherland. Friends call me Connie."

"Nice to meet you, Connie."

The woman's curious brown eyes softened. "How are you holding up?"

Here, in the bathroom, with no cameras around, Millie allowed herself to relax for a moment. To be herself with another competitor who might also need a break from the intense race. "I've had better days, but I've had worse ones, too."

"Same here." Connie smiled. "Are you and that groom fellow getting along?"

"Yes, we are," Millie admitted, feeling strangely at ease around Connie, who reminded Millie of her favorite teacher, Mrs. Cooper. "What about you and your teammate?"

Connie grimaced. "Well, we haven't killed each other yet."

"That doesn't sound too good."

"It's not especially since we're family. In-laws, actually. Her son married my daughter four years ago."

"So why aren't you getting along?" Millie asked.

"Her son married my daughter." Connie frowned. "Ava, my teammate, thinks her son could have done better than my daughter. She's made life difficult for everyone."

Ava sounded a lot like Millie's father. "I'm so sorry."

"It's Ava's loss, but it hurts my daughter. I can't stand that. Especially with grandkids involved."

"I don't blame you," Millie said. "It's never easy doing your best only to be told you're not good enough."

Connie sighed. "A woman her age should know better."

"Some people are set in their ways." Like Millie's father.

"I tell my girl a leopard can't change its spot and neither can Ava."

Millie wondered if her father would ever change. "One can still hope."

"That's true." Connie glanced around as if on a secret mission and trying to remain undercover. "Between you and me, I'm going to do everything in my power to make sure Ava doesn't win the million dollars."

"You plan to lose on purpose?" Millie whispered.

"To keep her from a million dollars? You betcha."

"But that would keep you from winning the money."

"I'd rather see her lose, than see me win." Connie winked. "Seriously I've got an adoring husband, a lovely, smart daughter, a great son-in-law and two beautiful grand-children. That's all I need."

"What about money to pay for your grandchildren's college?" Millie asked, not wanting Connie to regret her actions later.

The lines around the woman's mouth deepened. "I never thought about that."

"You might want to think about it."

"I will," Connie said. "Thanks."

"You're welcome."

"You know." Connie combed her hair with an orange comb. "I liked watching you on *The Groom,* Millie. You were different than the other women. I hope you do better this time around."

"Thanks." Millie grinned. "I hope I win."

"Well, you're going to have to be on top of your game with the partner you have. That groom fellow was an idiot for picking Desiree over you."

"She was a better pick for him than I would have been,"

Millie explained. "What you see on television isn't always a true representation of what's really going on."

Sometimes what she'd experienced during filming hadn't been a true representation, either. Just like during this race. The lines between reality and fantasy had a way of blurring with a camera capturing the action. The realization made Millie feel a little better.

"That's probably true." Connie pulled out her orange toothbrush. The show had gone overboard trying to make everything coordinate with team colors. "Just be careful. Your teammate can turn on the charm as easily as you can turn on that faucet there."

"He is charming. I won't deny that." Thinking about Jace handing over money to give to the little boy on the street filled Millie with warmth. "But he's also a nice guy, one who's smart, caring and dedicated to his family."

"Do you still like him?"

"He's my teammate." The words rushed from her mouth like water from a broken dam.

"Well, take away 'team,'" Connie said with a mischievous glint in her eyes. "And you've got 'mates.'"

"Trust me," Millie said. "Where Jace Westfall is concerned, the 'team' will never leave 'mates.'"

"Never say never," Connie cautioned with age-old wisdom.

"In this case, I know for a fact it will *never* happen."

The alarm clock on Jace's watch beeped. He kept his eyes closed and hit the snooze button.

The dream with Millie was too good to stop now. And then he remembered…

The race.

One million dollars.

Why was he dreaming about Millie when his dream was to win the money?

Jace bolted upright, aware of the unfamiliar scents and sounds around him.

"We're up for whatever they throw at us," said an athletic looking guy from the green team. "We might not get along and our mother might love him more than me, but we're still brothers and share the same blood. And let's be honest, a million bucks can sweep a whole lot of problems under the rug."

"I was hoping to get away from my wife's nagging for a month," a jovial fellow wearing red, who looked like he watched sports rather than participated in them, said. "But now we'll either save our marriage or end up on Divorce Court."

A buxom blond with collagen injected lips and dressed in purple smiled. "My teammate beat me for the title of Miss Galaxy U.S.A., but I'm not holding any grudges. You can't beat the exposure and if we win…"

Jace listened to the various tales. The casting director sure had done her job. All of the contestants had been set up. Each person had a story, and each was trying to make the best of the situation.

He wasn't sure which team had it worse being stuck with an unexpected partner, but Jace realized he and Millie had an advantage over the other pairs. They'd been through this before. That should make the race easier for them.

Then Jace remembered.

He'd rejected Millie. On national television. He still remembered the look of betrayal on her face, the disbelief.

The collar of his T-shirt tightened around his throat.

Millie might say she was over what happened, but was she really? He had seen the hesitation in her eyes. A couple of times she acted as if she didn't trust him.

That would make the race harder.

He would have to fix that.

Jace glanced at the cot next to his. Empty. No sign of a sleeping bag. Nothing.

His stomach clenched.

She didn't need him to take care of her like his mother and sisters, but the thought of her leaving without a word. Or worse, disappearing…

He noticed her sleeping bag and backpack on the floor near the foot of her cot.

She wasn't gone.

Jace blew out his breath.

Not that he'd been worried about her.

He hadn't. Okay, maybe a little.

She was his teammate. He couldn't race without her. That was the only reason he'd been concerned.

Jace knew better than to let Millie get to him. He wanted her at his side, not under his skin. Trying to develop a relationship in the middle of the race could be a deadly distraction. Not to mention a camera capturing every moment.

What if things didn't work out? Again. He could lose more than a million dollars.

"Good morning, Jace," Millie said behind him.

At the sound of her voice, heat flowed through his veins. Jace blew off the reaction. The outside temperature must be rising. Turning and seeing her for the first time that morning, his voice caught in his throat. He coughed. Hard.

Man, she looked good. Her short-sleeved shirt and quilted vest showed off her firm arms. Her blue shorts made her legs look so long. And what was up with her tousled hair? Millie didn't seem the type to want to look like some sex kitten.

Not that he cared, Jace reminded himself.

She was only his teammate.

T-E-A-M-M-A-T-E.

He focused on her running shoes. Sturdy. Good arch support. Double-knotted ties. His gaze drifted upward to her thin ankles and smooth calves.

"Did you sleep well?" she asked, her voice soft compared to the others in the large room sizing each other up.

Jace nodded. "You?"

"Yes." She shoved her zippered toiletry bag into her backpack. "I spoke with Derek and Matt."

No doubt the two guys must have loved that. They'd been flirting with Millie since meeting again in the gate area at LAX. "Did they give you any trouble?"

"They're harmless."

As harmless as a herd of hippos. "They want to distract you so you'll lose focus on the game."

"Maybe." She didn't sound convinced. "But the only thing they talked to me about was the pink team, who quit in San Francisco."

Everyone had been wondering about the pink team. Jace remembered one of the pinks from the start of his race, a thin brunette in her thirties who looked a bit desperate. "What happened?"

"No one knows, but it must have been bad for them to quit."

Guilt lodged in his throat. Jace had wanted Millie to quit. He was relieved she'd stayed. "Must have been."

"I guess we'll find out when we watch the show."

"The finale airs in December so you know what that means?"

Millie zipped her pack. "What?"

"Christmas in July."

"You're probably right." She adjusted a strap on her pack. The tightness of the strap matched the muscles across her upper back. "You know, there's going to be more pressure on today's race leg since no one wants to be the first team eliminated."

"Don't you mean 'canceled'?" he asked.

The show's producers used travel terms for different parts of the race. Instead of being eliminated, teams got canceled as if they were airline flights. They called the time between check-in and departure a layover. Tasks needing to be completed to earn clues were called delays.

"Canceled, eliminated." She hoisted her pack on her back. "Who cares as long as it's not us?"

"It won't be us."

"I'm ready." She adjusted the straps on her pack. "I'll meet you outside."

As she walked away, Jace noticed the bounce of hair and the sway of her hips. Still he admired her determination as much as the way she looked. Hell, she was ready to race before him. That was, in itself, amazing.

She stopped at the doorway, turned and smiled at him.

His mouth went dry.

Forget about Millie getting under his skin. He plopped onto his cot. She was already there. And he wanted—needed—her out. Out of his thoughts. Out of his sight. Out of his life.

Uh-oh. Jace had a problem. A really big problem.

* * *

"It won't be a problem," Jace told Millie on the bus ride from the remote town El Calafate in Patagonia.

They'd flown two and a half hours from Buenos Aires without incident. Now Millie stared out the window at the pine trees and snow-capped mountain peaks of The Argentina Glacier National Park and shivered. "I'm sorry, but I find the thought of trekking across a humongous piece of ice a bit overwhelming."

"It's the eighth wonder of the world, Freckles. That's what the guy at the airport said. Chances are it's no big deal." Jace tugged on the edge of her blue ski hat. "Even if it is, you won't be out there on your own. You're stuck with me, remember?"

"I know." And she was surprisingly thankful for that. Millie zipped up her jacket. "It's different having a teammate."

"*Cash Around the Globe* is a different kind of show than *The Groom*."

She crossed her fingers. "A better one."

"Much better," he said. "That whole dating setup..."

The disgust in his voice surprised her. "Not what you expected?" she asked.

"Not at all," he admitted. "I don't know how you competed against those other women, living together but not able to trust each other. That couldn't have been easy."

Especially with him as the jury and judge. Millie tapped down a rush of insecurity. "I made it through."

"And you'll make it through today, too." His eyes, as blue as the waters of Lake Argentine, met hers. "Only this time you won't have to do it alone."

Her throat thick with emotion, she nodded. This time around was different. But however real the challenges she and Jace faced together, they were still only participating on a reality television show. Millie couldn't forget that.

She didn't dare.

The bus slowed.

She glimpsed a wall of blue-white ice stretching as far as she could see out her window. The Perito Moreno Glacier. Her pulse picked up speed.

"We have no idea where any of the other teams are." Jace was on his feet with his pack strapped on his back before the bus stopped. "We have to cross quickly."

"I know."

All seven teams had flown from Guatemala City to Panama City to Buenos Aires. But there, the teams had scattered to make arrangements for the flight to El Calafate. The green and red teams had been on their plane, but hadn't caught the same bus.

That didn't mean they weren't on a different bus.

Or already on the glacier.

Millie pulled on her pack, and by the time she exited with the other passengers Jace held tickets for the boat ride that would take them to the glacier.

Holding onto the straps of her pack, she ran to the *Bajo de las Sombras* pier. The strong wind chilled her cheeks. She climbed aboard a ship with other tourists, who kept looking at Zack and Ryan with their equipment. A few people waved at the camera.

As the ship set sail, Jace gave Millie a thumbs-up. "We made it."

Her heart bumped.

Reality show, she reminded herself.

"The day's only beginning," she said. And that was after traveling some twenty hours to get here.

The ship maneuvered around bobbing icebergs. Millie shivered, either from the cold robbing body heat or fear at the enormity of the fifteen-story tower of blue ice in front of her.

"That thing is massive." Awe filled Jace's voice. "I wonder how big that sucker is under the water."

"I thought you said the glacier wasn't a big deal," she teased.

He raised a shoulder, smiling. "So I may have been wrong."

"You?" she asked. "Wrong?"

Jace stared at the milky-blue water surrounding the ship. "It's happened once or twice."

A smiled tugged on her lips. "That often?"

Twenty minutes later, Millie disembarked behind Zack and Ryan. Jace followed. A race flag led them to an Argentine park guide, who walked them around the bank of the lake and through a pine-scented forest to the glacier itself. The temperature seemed to drop, and the air felt wet.

"Are you warm enough?" Jace asked.

"Yes."

The guide gave them a short lecture on glacier formation and fitted them with crampons, spiked footwear that went over shoes to assist walking on ice, and instructed them how to walk. "Your clue is waiting for you on the glacier."

Millie looked over the ice and felt her stomach drop.

"How are you doing, Freckles?" Jace stepped onto the ice.

The crampons weighted her feet as the metal spikes on the toe and heel cut into the ice. She padded forward carefully to avoid ripping a hole in her pants leg or cutting herself. "I feel like a duck walking in these things," she confessed to both Jace and the camera.

"But at least we won't fall."

"Right."

Up and down they traveled, seeing every imaginable shade of blue. The ice was dirtier than she imagined it would be with rocks, pebbles and pools of water in some places. She felt like an ant who found itself on a strange blue-shaded ice sculpture.

The cracking and falling of a glacier piece breaking off and falling into the lake sounded like thunder.

A chill inched down Millie's spine. She glanced up at Jace. "Do you think it's safe?"

"Lots of tourists do this. We'll be fine." He gracefully made his way across the uneven surface. The glacier groaned and a piece the size of a house crumbled into the water. The birth of another iceberg. He showed no hesitation as he continued forward. "I won't let anything happen to you."

His confidence chipped away at her fear and soon she was enjoying the trek, awed by the ice formations and spectacular scenery surrounding her.

"You're doing great," Jace said.

"Thanks." She wished she could catch up to him, but she was going to be the tortoise to his hare today.

A few minutes later, he glanced back, his wide smile like a little boy attending his first professional baseball game. "Isn't this incredible?"

"I don't know how we'll top this one."

As Millie stared at him, an iceberg-size lump lodged in her throat. Jace looked so comfortable and strong out here on this massive slab of blue ice she had to look away before she did or said something stupid.

"Me, either," he admitted.

Their guide pointed out a crevasse in the ice, something she'd rather not have seen. Still Millie continued on.

A staircase had been hacked out of the ice. She followed Jace up the steps and found herself on the top of the glacier.

"Hey, there's somebody waving a race flag," he shouted back. "They must have the clue pouches."

"I'll be right there." He'd been ahead of her since they hit the ice, and she expected him to run ahead and get the pouch, but Jace stayed where he was until she caught up to him.

"Why didn't you get the clue?" she asked.

"I wanted to wait for you." He stuck a strand of hair back into her ski hat. "Teammates, right?"

His words and actions were strictly platonic. That's what Millie wanted, but she couldn't deny a twinge of disappointment. She smiled wanly. "Yes, teammates."

"Let's go."

She took a step. Her right crampon caught on her left pant leg, and she tripped. Gasped.

Strong arms grabbed her before she hit the ice. "I've gotcha, Freckles."

Jace. She stared up at him. His body hard. His breath hot. "T-thanks."

"You okay?"

No. Her heart raced. She couldn't breathe. Millie nodded, ignoring Zack and Ryan who filmed the entire exchange.

As the guide checked her leg to make sure she hadn't cut herself, Jace held onto her. "Sure? You're a little pale."

That was better than blushing like a teenager with a crush on the most popular guy in school. "I'm okay. Really."

"All good," the guide said. *"Vamos."*

Millie hesitated.

Jace laced his gloved fingers with hers, and she felt a little hitch to her heart. "Come on."

Together they received their clue pouch. He pulled out a "DELAY" card. "You read it."

She took the card. "The tango is a matter of national pride for residents of Buenos Aires. Fly back to Buenos Aires and find Casa Las Tanguerias on Avenida Balcarce where you will learn the steps to this expressive, passionate dance. As you dance with your teammate, a panel of expert tango dancers will judge your dance and determine whether you have earned your clue. If not, you must practice before trying again."

"Do you dance?" Jace asked.

Millie's stomach dropped. "I've taken dance lessons, but the tango wasn't one of the steps I learned."

"What dances did you do?"

She cleared her dry throat. "All the proper dances young women are suppose to do at a cotillion."

"You were a debutante?"

"No," she said. "For once, my father listened to me and agreed I would have only made a fool of myself."

And by default, him.

"You would have been a cute deb."

She shrugged off his words, but the compliment still warmed her cold insides.

"I took a ballroom dance class in college, but that was a long time ago," Jace said. "Though the all guy teams will have a problem with this task."

Millie laughed. "Can you imagine Derek and Matt doing the tango together?"

"No, but I bet they could sell tickets for that one."

"I'm sure they could," she said. "The women teams won't have as big a problem as the men teams. A lot of men don't dance so women are used to dancing together."

"Dancing's not really a guy thing."

"But women love a man who can dance."

Jace drew his brows together. "All women?"

"Pretty much."

He thought for a moment. "Even you?"

"What do you think?" she asked.

Jace tucked the card into his jacket pocket. "We need to get off this giant ice cube and tango."

CHAPTER SIX

"I'M SORRY," one of the tango judges said in accented English. "You did not earn the clue."

Millie clutched Jace's hand tighter. He squeezed back reassuringly.

"Sure, we did." Okay, fine, the first time they'd danced, they'd both messed up, but this time...

He ran the steps through his head. *El Paseo. La cadencia. Salida. La resolucìon.* They'd walked, turned, stopped and added an embellishment, a *zarendeo* also known as a shake. No stumbles, no stepping on toes, no mistakes.

"We did everything we were supposed to."

Including traveling counterclockwise on the dance floor.

The beautiful female judge stood and tossed her long black hair.

"The tango is not about steps. It's a dance of improvisation." She sashayed toward them. "You must take what you learned from the instructors and make the dance your own."

"Our own?" he asked.

"Sì."

His gaze collided with Millie's. She didn't seem to understand any better than he did.

Next door, he could hear two of the other teams practicing. They had to get out of here. But...

"How do we make the dance our own?" Millie asked.

"Feel the music. Experience the emotion." The two male judges nodded their agreement. The woman closed her eyes, swaying. "Let your steps express those feelings. Only then will you discover *el alma del tango*. The soul of the tango."

That sounded...

"Impossible," Millie mumbled.

The woman shook her head. "Not impossible."

"Can you be a little more specific?" Millie asked.

"How about a lot more specific," Jace muttered.

"Hold your partner closer. Her chest pressed to yours."

Some of Jace's frustration seeped away as he admired the cleavage shown by Millie's low-cut dress. "I can do that."

"You also need to loosen up." The woman unbuttoned his blue silk shirt. "This might help."

Great. He grimaced. With the silk and billowy sleeves and open neck, all he needed were hair gel and gold chains around his neck to look like a gigolo.

Millie smiled. "It does look better."

"And you." The woman faced her. "You look beautiful."

Jace agreed. Millie wore high heels and a sexy shimmering blue dress. The slits up the sides swirled around her legs and provided welcome glimpses of her thigh.

"But like your partner, you are too stiff," the woman continued. "Loosen up. Move to the music. Not just your feet and hips, but your entire body. Let the beat match *tu corazón*."

"My heart," Millie repeated.

"Allow your heart to be your guide," the judge said. "Understand?"

Millie nodded.

"Attitude is everything in the tango. If you think you're a good dancer, you'll be good. The man uses his *machismo* and sets the tone." The woman pulled one of the male judges from his chair. "You, *chica,* follow his lead. Watch."

The woman cued the music. The pair danced around the floor of the dark and smoky tango bar, and Jace understood what she'd been trying to say. The two stopped in the center of the dance floor. The few patrons sitting around round tables clapped. According to their dance instructors the place didn't start filling up until after midnight, and it was only eleven now.

"The tango is a conversation without words," the woman judge said. "Let your movements communicate."

"Communicate what?" Millie asked.

"Emotion," the woman purred. "Passion. Sex."

Sex, huh? Jace could handle that.

Except Millie didn't seem too keen on the idea.

She blushed. "Um, thanks."

"Go practice." The woman smoothed her skirt. *"Buena suerte."*

Jace opened the door to the practice room. They were going to need more than luck to pull this off.

Millie seemed to be limping. She leaned her back against a wall, her right foot not touching the ground.

"What's wrong with your foot?"

"Blisters."

From their trek across the glacier? Or the hours they'd put in practicing the damn dance?

"Let me see."

Straightening, she didn't put weight on her foot. "It's fine."

"They have a first-aid kit," he said. "Don't be a martyr. We still have a long way to go."

"I won't slow you down."

"I don't want you to hurt."

She removed her shoe. "There's one on my heel and one on the ball of my foot."

Kneeling, he held onto her ankle. Her skin felt so soft. He was eye level to one of the slits in her dress. He followed it up.

Damn, she had long legs.

Nice legs. Smooth.

Millie lost her balance and grabbed onto his shoulder. "Sorry."

He released her ankle, stood and picked her up in his arms.

Her eyes widened. "What are you doing?"

Jace placed her on a chair. "You'll be more comfortable."

And he wouldn't be in a position to look up her damn dress.

He placed moleskin and a bandage on each of her blisters. "This will get you through the practice and performance."

"Thanks, but…" She hung her head. "I don't know if I can do all the things she said."

He raised her chin with his fingertip. "We have to give this our best shot."

"I've been trying my hardest."

"I know." Jace knew she was tired and hurting. He didn't blame Millie for her doubts. Hell, he was exhausted himself. Not to mention feeling like an idiot in his costume. That gave him an idea. "So what if you don't do them?"

Her forehead wrinkled. "You just said—"

"Let's not be Millie and Jace dancing, but Evita and Rico."

She laughed.

Good. That was the reaction he'd wanted.

"Seriously, Freckles, you're dressed to the nines and I could give Rico Suave a run for the money in my getup," he explained. "Trust me."

A beat passed. And another.

Millie pursed her lips with a haughtiness he'd never seen before. One that hit him low and hard, promising things he could only imagine. She flipped her hair back. "Don't you mean Evita?"

"Third time's the charm," Jace—make that Rico—murmured, as he placed his hand on her back.

Millie hoped so. She clasped her right hand with his.

Dancing in front of the judges and camera had been hard enough the first two times. Now with patrons, people who knew how to tango, in the bar sipping drinks and watching them, and her foot throbbing with pain, she didn't know if she could do this.

She didn't have to, she reminded herself.

Evita did.

Evita could.

Millie took a deep breath, something hard to do in the tight fitting dress she wore. The plunging neckline and slits on the side left little to the imagination. Not that the men staring at her seemed to mind. Or Jace.

She looked up at him, handsome in his flowing blue silk shirt and black slacks and shoes. "Let's show 'em what we've got, Evita."

He pulled her close, her chest pressing against his. He might look cool and calm, but the rapid tattoo of his heart told Millie he was nervous, too. She took comfort she wasn't the only one.

All she had to do was remember what the judge had told

them. Feel the music. Follow his moves. Communicate emotion with motion.

Listening to the opening strains of the song, she focused on Jace. Something shattered near the bar. Millie bit her lip.

He winked.

She forced a smile.

"Remember, it takes two to tango," he whispered in her ear, his warm breath, a caress against her neck, sending tingles racing through her.

He stared at her as if she was the only woman in the world and he wanted her.

Bad.

She gulped.

Evita wouldn't gulp. She would…

Millie raised her chin, puckered her lips and kissed the air next to his cheek. "For luck."

His eyes darkened. His jaw tensed. She sensed the tension in his arms.

Evita wouldn't make it easy for him. She would taunt, tantalize, tease.

She lifted her chin, arched her back to align her hips with his. Her breasts thrust forward, pressing closer against him.

"How badly do you want it, Rico?" she whispered.

At his sharp intake of breath, she turned her head quickly away from him.

The show had begun.

He took a step forward with his left foot. She stepped back with her right. Around the floor they moved.

He stalked like a panther on the hunt for his prey. Aggression, power, passion.

The music seeped inside of her, the rhythm flowing through her body like the blood in her veins.

The steps melded as emotion took control of the motion. His fiery gaze locked on her.

She shimmied, turned and twisted away from him. He was going to have to work harder if he wanted to catch her.

Pulling her to him again, he rocked back so her chest lay across his. Heat burned between them. She pressed her cheek against his.

Time stopped for an instant.

Then she was back on her feet moving away. His confidence and strength were contagious. But he didn't let her get far from him. He pulled her close. She went willingly, wrapping her right leg around his hips and leg. He spun them around.

Closer and closer.

Triumph filled his eyes. He thought he had her.

Not yet.

She turned her head away sharply and moved away from him.

The chase continued around and around the dance floor until the music came to an end.

Slowly he lowered her into a dip until she was practically horizontal. His face was mere inches from hers. Sweat beaded on his forehead. Her breath quickened.

Millie parted her lips to thank him, but Jace covered her open mouth with his. And kissed her.

She tasted salt and heat. The way he moved his mouth over hers sent fire rushing through her veins.

His strong hands held her in place. A good thing, too, because her legs, as solid as melted butter, could have never supported her.

But that didn't stop her from kissing him back.

Her left hand splayed across his hip. She arched to meet

him, eager to taste more of him. Her response made him deepen the kiss more.

Pleasure exploded through her body like the grand finale of a fireworks display. Only this wasn't the end. If anything his kiss felt like the beginning, the start of something...lasting.

He'd never kissed her like this before. No man had.

Millie didn't want the kiss to stop. He kissed her as if he couldn't get enough of her, as if she were the air he needed to breathe.

Forget about protecting her heart. She was willing to risk everything for more kisses. She wanted him to feel how she felt.

Pressing closer against him, she moved her lips over his with an eagerness she'd never experienced before.

Clapping and cheering erupted, breaking the mood.

Jace raised his head to look at their audience. Straightening, he pulled Millie to her feet and twirled her to take their bow.

Flushed, embarrassed, aroused, she clutched his hand, seeking reassurance in his eyes. Her insides shook, but she kept a smile on her face.

For the patrons. For the judges. For the camera.

"Great performance, Freckles," Jace said, not meeting her eyes.

Her lips bruised, her breathing ragged and her resolve completely shattered, she felt as if someone had dumped a container of ice water on her, jolting her awake from a deep sleep.

Her smile wobbled. "You, too."

That had to be why he kissed her, performing for the camera in order to earn the clue.

Part of the show, Millie told herself. Evita and Rico. No different from *The Groom* and his brides the last time around.

Unfortunately that realization didn't make her feel any better. His previous kisses hadn't affected her this way. They'd been more like pecks compared to the way he'd just devoured her on the dance floor.

Why had his kisses changed? Millie fought the urge to touch her throbbing lips. That's what she needed to understand. Nothing had changed between them. Unless…unless he'd kissed her on the rebound. And if that were true…

All three judges stood and clapped. A standing ovation, but Millie didn't care. She was more concerned with protecting herself and her suddenly vulnerable heart.

The gorgeous female judge handed Jace a familiar looking clue pouch. Her red glossed lips curved into a sexy smile. "Now that's how to communicate emotion. I felt your passion—" her closed fist pounded her heart "—here."

Millie felt it, too.

Like a knife.

And she never wanted to feel that way again.

Sitting in a famous steakhouse, a converted warehouse with wood paneled walls and an open fire grill, Jace stared across the table at Millie.

His temperature shot up at the memory of his lips against hers. He sipped from his water glass.

It was just a kiss. It wasn't even the first time he'd kissed her. But those kisses during *The Groom* had been tentative, almost polite. He'd always been careful with Millie on that show, tried to act the part of a gentleman, knowing how nervous she was, not wanting to hurt her.

This time, all he could think about was really kissing her and tasting her lips. He'd never expected her response.

Talk about a spin-his-world-off-its-axis kiss.

He shook it off.

The moment. That was all it had been.

He'd gotten wrapped up in the dance. Besides he hadn't been kissing Millie. He'd been kissing Evita.

"Thirsty," Millie asked.

He nodded. "Long day."

"True, but you might not want to drink too much." She fiddled with her white napkin. "We have no idea what they'll make us eat."

In order to get their next clue, he and Millie were going to have to eat whatever was served.

"As long as it's not crawling off the plate," he said, watching Zack circle the table with his camera. "I'll be fine."

"Me, too." Millie's gaze met his then she stared at the table. "Fine, that is."

Jace tried reconciling the woman across from him to the one he'd danced with earlier. In her blue warm-up suit that covered every inch of skin except her face, neck and hands, Millie looked nothing like the woman at the tango bar. She acted nothing like her, either.

"*Parilladas.*" A uniformed waiter placed the biggest platter of barbecued meat Jace had ever seen in the center of the table. Next came a bowl of sauce. "*Chimichurri.*"

"*Gracias,*" Millie said. As soon as the waiters left, she bit her lip. "How are we going to eat all this?"

"One bite at a time." Suddenly eating a seventy-two ounce sirloin in an hour for a free meal at Big Texan Steak Ranch in Amarillo seemed more like snacking. "At least it's cooked and smells good."

But not as good as Millie.

Stop. Now.

Jace had to think of Millie only as his teammate, not a beautiful, desirable woman who'd surprised the hell out of him tonight. She was not Evita.

"The sooner we start this—" Millie placed a slab of meat on her plate "—the sooner we get the clue and get out of here."

He did the same. "Don't forget the *chimichurri*. Sauce might help."

"Do you recognize everything?" she asked.

Jace stared on the platter. Sweetbreads, kidneys, udders. Maybe even a bull testicle or two. He gulped. "I don't think we're supposed to recognize all of it."

Millie ate her first piece. "The meat's good."

"So is the sauce. It has a bite to it."

"You like spicy things?"

He thought back to the tango bar. "Yeah, I do."

She spooned sauce onto her plate. "Me, too."

He speared another piece of meat and dropped the chunk on his plate. They ate in silence. One by one, teams joined them at the steakhouse. The purple beauties. The red marrieds. The orange grannies.

"None of the guys are here," Millie said.

"Good." Jace wiped his mouth. "The males teams are going to be our toughest competition. With the exception of the yellow team."

She held her water glass in midair. "The two brainy guys?"

"You mean geeks."

Millie sighed. "Liking *Star Wars* doesn't make you a geek."

"Reciting lines from the movies and professing your religion to be Jedi does."

"They are nice."

Jace took another piece from the platter. "I wonder what caused their friendship to splinter. Did someone cross over to the Dark Side?"

"Close," Millie said. "An authentic Darth Vader helmet was up for auction, and one beat the other for it."

Jace laughed. "You're kidding."

"I'm not." She wiped her hands on her napkin. "It's still a point of contention between them, and they're worried it'll affect how they do in the race."

"Well, if there's something you ever want that badly, just tell me and I'll let you have it."

"I will. Thanks." Smiling, she spooned more sauce on her plate. "And if you want to eat the rest of the meat, feel free."

He laughed. "What do you know about the other teams?"

"Well, the red team over there has been having marriage difficulties. Karen thinks this race will make or break them. She's really worried."

"What about the blondes?" he asked.

"They want to be actresses or models," Millie said. "They hope this show is their big break."

Like Desiree. "Sounds familiar."

Millie reached over the table and touched his arm. "I'm so sorry. You must miss her."

"Miss who?" he asked.

"Desiree."

"No." The odd thing was, he didn't. She'd hurt his pride. She hadn't touched his heart. "What about the orange team?"

Millie pulled back her hand and picked up her water. "I like Connie. She's decided to put whatever money she wins in a college fund for her grandkids."

"What about the other orange granny?"

Millie bit into another piece of meat.

Interesting. Jace had sized the other teams up as threats or nothing to worry about. He hadn't given much thought to them as people. Not the way she had.

Jace realized he'd done the same with the women on *The Groom*. He'd sized them up as having the qualities he'd wanted in a wife or not. He hadn't really gotten to know them as individuals.

Millie wiped sauce from her fingers.

If she was Evita, he could reach across the table and suck the sauce off her fingers for her. Millie, however, would misinterpret the action, thinking it meant something more than it did.

"What?" she asked.

"Nothing. Ready for another piece?"

Slowly the pile of meat disappeared. Jace had never felt so full in his life. He leaned back in his chair his stomach full and bloated. For the first time in his life, he saw the appeal of being a vegetarian.

In spite of his physical discomfort, the tension between he and Millie had eased.

She groaned. "I don't think I can eat another bite."

Four pieces remained. "We're almost finished."

"Almost being the operative word." She took an odd-shaped piece of meat. "I don't think I want to know what this is."

Jace eyed it. Testicles. "No, you don't."

She chewed anyway.

What a woman. Teammate, he corrected, and bit into another piece himself.

"You have sauce on your cheek," Millie said.

He wiped his face with a napkin.

"It's still there."

"Where?" he asked.

She pointed to her right cheek.

He raised the napkin back to his face.

"Other side."

Jace rubbed his left cheek. "Better."

"You missed it. Try an inch from where you were."

He did.

"Over to the left. My left. Now down. A little more."

How could they dance together, but not be able to get sauce off his face? He tossed the napkin on his lap. "Forget about it."

She leaned over the table and wiped his cheek with her own napkin. "It's gone."

"Thanks."

He concentrated on the remaining pieces of meat, the ache in his belly matching the pain at his temple. He liked being touched like that.

If only Evita were doing the touching. She was the kind of woman who came with no strings. Unlike Millie who came with so many strings she could tie him up like a Christmas present.

Jace wasn't ready for that. He didn't know if he ever would be. He had so much on his plate with his mother, sisters and business. He wouldn't be able to give Millie what she needed. What she deserved.

He'd only end up disappointing her. Hurting her. Again.

He couldn't let that happen. He wouldn't.

The clue sent them back to the airport's international terminal. Sleep-deprived and overfed, Millie needed to concentrate on the task at hand, but she kept thinking about

Jace. He didn't miss Desiree. That meant he hadn't kissed Millie on the rebound. That meant the kiss had been an act, a way to complete the tango delay.

She could accept that.

Because by going that extra step, the two of them had become a real team, not simply two people put together by a ratings-hungry television show. They were stronger together than apart. Even Jace had to see that now.

Outside in the pitch-blackness of three o'clock in the morning, Millie scrambled out of the cab and ran inside the International Terminal. She saw the Aerolineas Argentinas sign and heard the noise from a vacuum or floor polisher, but that was it. No workers. No other teams. No race banners.

Jace grabbed her hand and started running.

"Wha…" She saw the race banner, the mat with a red line following their path into South America and Colt standing there with one his habitual deadpanned expression.

A check-in at the airport? Millie hadn't been expecting that. She ran faster. Each step hurt her blistered foot, but she didn't care. She hit the mat at the same time as Jace.

"Millie and Jace," Colt said with no emotion to his voice. "You are team number one!"

"Yes." She jumped and caught Jace's gaze with her own. Something passed between them. An electrical surge. A sort of static charge. A memory of what had happened at the tango bar. A sudden urge to hug him was strong, but she slapped both of his hands with hers instead. "We did it."

"Good job, Freckles."

"You, too."

Colt grinned as if he already knew the show would be a Top Ten hit. "This show isn't called *Cash Around the Globe* for nothing. Your team has won twenty thousand dollars for placing first on the second leg of the race."

Millie gasped. "Twenty thousand."

"Dollars," Jace said. He gave her a quick hug.

She missed his warmth and his scent when he let go of her. Boy, she must be more tired than she thought.

"There is no layover between legs two and three. You can rest here at the airport and sleep on the flight," Colt explained, handing her a clue pouch. "Good luck."

Luck? What they needed was a shower, clean clothes and sleep. Still she'd just won ten thousand dollars for her school. She really couldn't complain.

Millie unzipped the pouch and pulled out the clue card.

"Say adios to Buenos Aires and fly to Cape Town, South Africa," she read. "Take a taxi to the Table Top cableway station. Ride the cable car to the top where you will follow the flags to your next task. Be ready for the thrill of a lifetime. You have fifty dollars for this leg of the race."

"We might have a long wait ahead of us." Jace moved in front of a closed ticket counter and removed his backpack. "I'll stay here and you can wash up. Then we can switch."

"Thank you."

"For what?"

The corners of her mouth lifted. "For being a really great teammate."

CHAPTER SEVEN

"So MUCH for going into Cape Town with a lead," Jace said.

After napping on an airport floor in Buenos Aires for a few hours, they had flown to São Paulo, Brazil, with three other teams—red, orange, purple. All eight racers waited to board the same flight to Johannesburg.

From first place to tied for fourth.

Funny, but Millie didn't seem upset most of the teams had caught up to them. If the smile on her face was any indication, she enjoyed the interaction with the other contestants especially the woman from the orange team sitting next to her.

"It could be worse," the woman in orange said. "All the teams could be here."

The others laughed.

Good point, Jace realized. At least he and Millie had twenty grand to show for their efforts in Argentina. Taxes would take a chunk out of the money, but what remained would help his business and Millie's students.

He stared at her. Curly hair stuck out from the blue baseball cap she wore. She looked cute. Sweeter. More innocent. An urge to protect her grew inside of him.

Nah. That's what guys did. He'd spent most of his life looking out for his mom and sisters. This was nothing new.

Except his feelings weren't the least brotherly.

"I keep wondering where the other teams are," Millie said.

"All of the boys had trouble dancing," the woman in orange said.

Nicole, one of the blondes from the purple team, nodded. "We were the last to leave the steakhouse, and none of the guys had shown up."

"We're showing up now," a male voice said.

Matt and Derek, dressed in black, walked over. The green team, brothers Bay and Lake, followed them.

"No more yellow team," Millie said, sadness filling her voice.

"Those geeks never made it to the restaurant." Lake, a big, tall jock type who owned a sports bar, snickered. "They got canceled right in the tango bar."

Millie sighed. "They were so nice."

The other blonde from the purple team named Krystal agreed.

"They were nice guys, and they tried." Matt pushed his way through the group and squeezed in beside Millie and the woman wearing orange. "But they never could find the beat. And without the right beat—"

"You're not going to get it done," Derek finished for him.

Millie retied her tennis shoes and double-knotted them. Jace wondered how her blisters were doing, but he couldn't ask and betray a possible weakness to the other teams.

"Beat or not, learning to tango wasn't easy," she said. "We had to dance three times to earn the clue."

"We were three, too," Krystal said.

"Four for us," the red team wife said. "I couldn't believe how hard dancing the tango was."

"It was harder for two geeks who couldn't dance. Not even the Force could help them tango," Lake said.

The green and black teams laughed, but no one joined in.

"Maybe if they'd been dancing to the Imperial Death March, they would have been able to do it." Bay hummed a few bars of the famous movie theme. "Or the cantina song."

The two guy teams continued laughing and poking fun at the yellow team.

Millie stared at the carpet, her mouth tight.

Jace wanted the guys to shut up. He might have called the two guys geeks, but they didn't deserve to be humiliated on national television or made fun of by these bozos. It wasn't as if either green or black had finished in the top of the pack.

"So how was it dancing the tango together, guys?" Jace asked. "Who wore the dress?"

The appreciative gleam in Millie's eyes was worth more than whatever payback his questions would bring.

Both the green and black teams glared at him.

"We got the clue," Lake said. "That's what matters."

Lou, the husband from the red team, released a belly laugh loud enough to echo through the waiting area. "Guess we know who wore the pants on your team."

Ignoring the play-by-play, Matt scooted closer to Millie. "I just wish I could have seen you in one of those sexy dresses. I bet you looked hot."

"Gorgeous," one of the orange team said.

Millie blushed. "Thanks."

"I wish I could have kept my dress," Nicole said wistfully.

"One of the bartenders said you and the groom dude danced well," Matt added.

Groom dude? Jace's grit his teeth. "I have a name."

Matt didn't seem to hear him. All the guy's attention was focused on Millie. Not that Jace blamed him, but it was a little weird seeing other men flirt with his...his teammate.

She stretched her arms over her head and rolled her shoulders. Tired or sore? Jace wondered. Probably both after the past twenty-four hours they'd had.

"Shoulders hurt?" Derek asked.

"From running with the backpack, I think." She patted the floor. "And sleeping on this."

Derek stepped between the contestants and sat behind a surprised looking Millie. "I'll fix you right up."

Much to the dismay of a peeved looking Matt and the surprise of an also peeved Jace, she leaned forward. "Thanks."

With a smug grin, Derek massaged her shoulders. "How does that feel?"

The look of pure pleasure on Millie's face hit Jace right in the solar plexus. She moaned. "Perfect."

He would show her perfect. Right after he punched Derek, whose hands were all over Millie. And not just her shoulders. Every muscle in Jace's body tensed.

Derek whispered something in her ear. Millie giggled.

What was going on? Why was she letting some random guy get so close to her? Good question. Jace inched forward in his chair. She never let him touch her like that on *The Groom*. Not that he'd tried. Maybe he should have offered to rub her shoulders himself.

But he knew Millie was anxious and not very confident with men. She wasn't used to the kind of games men and women played. She was a nice girl.

She hadn't danced like a nice girl when she'd been playing Evita. She hadn't kissed like a nice girl, either.

Forget about it.

A massage on the airport floor in front of all the teams, cameramen and audio guys and other passengers meant nothing.

Still it bugged him. So much so he couldn't look away.

"Do your shoulders hurt, Jace?" Krystal asked.

At least he thought her name was Krystal, not Nicole. The two beauty pageant contestants with California beach blond good looks and made-for-bikini bodies seemed inter-changeable. "No."

Krystal pressed her shoulders back so her D-cup breasts stuck out further. "Mine do."

"Try stretching." He flicked his gaze from her chest to her face. "Rolling your shoulders might help, too."

Krystal pouted.

Jace glanced at Millie to see if she noticed. She had her eyes half-closed and an expression of pure contentment on her face. She'd never looked at him like that.

"Want me to rub your shoulders, Krystal?" Lake asked.

"That would be wonderful." The blonde flashed the man in green a wide smile. Making her way to Lake, she stared down her nose at Jace. "Just because you were raised with a silver spoon doesn't make you better than any of us."

Eyes open, Millie sat rim-rod straight.

Jace looked at Krystal. "Is that what you think?"

The blond beauty queen nodded. "You know, Daddy's portfolio and a mansion in the nicest area in town."

"No."

"Penthouse apartment over looking Central Park?"

"Sorry. Try Shady Oaks Trailer Park instead." The sudden silence was deafening. He stood. "Anyone want something to drink?"

A chorus of nos answered him, except for one yes from Millie's friend on the orange team. The older woman handed him a couple of dollar bills. "I'd like a bottle of water, Jace."

"Sure thing…" He tried to remember her name.

"Connie. The other orange granny is Ava."

Ava rolled her eyes. "How many times do I have to tell you we are not the orange grannies?"

"Water it is, Connie," Jace said.

As he made his way to an airport shop, footsteps sounded behind him. A random passenger he hoped.

"Jace. Wait." Millie caught up to him. Zack was right behind her with camera in hand. "I'll go with you."

"I can get you a water."

"I want to go with you." She walked next to him.

"Suit yourself."

She followed him into the shop. "You never told me where you grew up."

Grabbing two bottles from the shelf, he shrugged, aware of the camera focused on them.

Millie had grown up rich. She was used to the finer things in life even if she didn't choose to live that lifestyle now. She couldn't understand.

"So what else haven't you told me about yourself, Jace Westfall?" Her tone teased, but her eyes were serious.

He didn't want her pity, but he couldn't afford to have this come between them, either. Not with the race at stake. "Nothing I'm going to admit on camera."

"Later?"

Damn. She wasn't going to let it drop.

He didn't want to admit weakness.

He never wanted to go back to that time. Not ever.

"Jace?" she pressed.

"Later."

"The camera's off." Millie double-checked her seat belt as the airplane taxied down the runway. "Will you talk to me now?"

"What do you want to know?" he asked.

Everything. She would bet growing up in Shady Oaks Trailer Park was only a small piece of a larger puzzle. "Whatever you want to tell me."

"Can I ask you a question first?"

Millie covered herself with a blanket. "What?"

"What's going on with you and the black team?" he asked.

"Nothing."

A muscle twitched at his jaw. "Matt didn't look too happy about you and Derek."

"Me and Derek?"

"You two looked pretty cozy back there."

"Cozy." Millie laughed, both embarrassed and touched by his…concern. "You sound almost jealous?"

"Why would I be jealous?" he answered quickly.

"No reason." She brushed aside a twinge of disappointment. "I mean, we're just teammates."

"That's right."

Still, tension built between them. Millie didn't want that.

"Nothing is going on with me and the black team," she said. "Matt's like a big, cute puppy."

"Cute?"

Not as cute as Jace. "Well, if you like that dark, athletic, paramedic type."

"And you do?"

His one question was turning into several. Millie didn't

know whether to feel flattered or annoyed. She was supposed to be learning about him. "Sometimes."

Jace's nostril flared. "What about Derek?"

"My shoulders hurt. He's a physical therapist. He made me feel better. End of story."

"So what did you want me to tell you?" Jace asked.

"I'd like to know more about your childhood," she admitted.

He stared at the seat pocket in front of him. "My dad left us when I was eight. He took everything worth anything. As soon as the divorce papers were signed, we never saw him again. My mom never received a penny of child support, either."

Millie's heart ached for him. No wonder he felt such a responsibility to his family. "What did you all do?"

"We sold whatever was left, but still couldn't make the rent." No emotion entered his voice. He spoke as if everyone had grown up like this or the experience had happened to someone else. "We got evicted, and were living in an old Buick when my uncle gave my mom the trailer. Welcome to Shady Oaks Trailer Park. I still remember the old sign with this giant oak tree with two robins on it."

Millie felt like she'd been hit over the head with a big stick. "You lived in a car?"

He winced. "It wasn't by choice."

"I know that, but I want to understand."

Telling her this had to be hard on Jace. Millie was angry with herself for putting him through this. She was also angry with herself for fantasizing during *The Groom* about a future with a man she never really knew. One who hadn't trusted her with the truth about how he'd grown up. Not that she blamed him.

Not at all.

"You do what you have to do," he explained. "My mom took a job at a company's cafeteria and worked her way up to executive secretary."

"Why didn't you say anything?"

"It's not something you broadcast to the world."

Pride. He'd kept the truth hidden from her on purpose. He hadn't been playing a role for the camera; he'd been playing a role all his life. The big protector of his family, the big success with his own business. He didn't want to be seen as less than a man, someone who couldn't care for his family.

"Look how far you've come," she said. "You started with nothing and became a success."

"A success might be pushing it."

"It's not." She respected all he'd accomplished and knew others would, too. "You would be a great role model. Especially for kids in similar situations."

"If I save my company, I'll think about that."

"Please do," she urged.

The fasten seat belt light illuminated.

"I'm going to sleep." With that, he closed his eyes.

Millie stared at Jace as if seeing him for the first time. And she was. He'd trusted her with himself. She couldn't have been more happy. Even if it was only so they could win the race. That was enough.

In Cape Town, Millie hopped out of the cab at Table Mountain's lower cableway station on Tafelburg Road. Jace was at her heels. Exactly as they'd planned.

Zack cursed as he carried the camera.

Ryan struggled to catch up to them. "What's gotten into you guys?"

Millie exchanged a secret smile with Jace.

"Teamwork," she said, glancing back.

She'd thought they'd been working as a team, but there had never been this same rapport before. There had never been the same trust.

What Jace had told her had changed everything. For the better.

They'd managed to leave the red and orange teams, who had flown with them from Johannesburg, in the dust. They were in the lead and not about to lose it.

The four of them entered the cable car along with thirty others. The car whisked them to the summit, rotating as it ascended to give passengers a full view of the city below. Hanging from wires didn't give her a warm and fuzzy feeling so she didn't look out the large glass windows.

Jace leaned forward. "We're almost at the top."

"I'm ready."

And she was.

Outside, Millie zipped her fleece-lined jacket to combat the cold breeze. Standing on solid ground, she could finally enjoy the panorama of the city sprawl, jutting peaks of stone and an island in the middle of a carpet of blue water.

"We're standing three thousand feet up."

"That's nothing compared to where we've been."

He laughed. "The race marker is over here."

They ran past tourists and hikers. About sixty feet away, a race banner blew. Several people stood around.

"This is it," Jace said.

Millie looked at the harnesses, rope and helmets.

If by some miracle you're not eliminated right away, they will want you to jump out of an airplane or climb a mountain. Neither of which you have the courage to do.

Her father's words and the sinking feeling in her stomach were nothing compared to what lay below her— pure vertical drop down to waves crashing against rocks. She swallowed.

"Who wants to abseil first?" asked a guide with a distinct British accent.

Abseil? What was that? Hope filled her. Maybe she wasn't going to have to go over the edge. "What does abseil mean?"

"Rappel, love," the guide explained. "You'll wear a harness that attaches to a rope and go down to the bottom where you'll find your next clue."

The blood rushed from her head. She felt light-headed. She closed her eyes. "Oh, boy."

Jace touched her shoulder. "You can do this."

"My father said I was a coward."

Jace stared at her steadily. "Your father's wrong. You're one of the bravest people I know."

"Thank you." His words gave her strength. She opened her eyes. That sure was a long way down. "But I'm not into, um, extreme stuff like that. I prefer to have both feet on the ground. Unless surrounded by lots of metal and strapped securely in a seat with a flotation device nearby."

"I know you don't like heights."

"Understatement of the year," she muttered.

He gave her a reassuring squeeze. She wished he'd hold her instead.

"You've got more heart than anyone I know."

"Thanks, but my heart and I are addicted to breathing."

He laughed. "We all are."

"A little fear is natural." The guide held out a harness.

"It's a pure adrenaline rush. The thrill of a lifetime, but it's a controlled descent. Very safe."

Jace stepped forward. "I'll go first."

"Does that mean you'll catch me if I fall?" she asked, trying to sound lighthearted.

"I'll do my best."

The guide outfitted him with a harness, gloves and helmet. A few instructions, and the guide walked Jace around some boulders where he was clipped onto a rope. He stood on the edge, looking like a model from an outdoor magazine. If only this were for a photo shoot and not the real thing…

"See." He held his gloved hands palms up in the air. "Nothing to it."

She felt sick to her stomach. "Good luck."

As Zack and his camera stayed on top with her, Jace disappeared. No doubt, the show had planned for other cameras to be set-up along the route. The guide shouted out something.

Millie was too frightened to listen or watch. She focused on the breathtaking view around her, looking into the distance, past the city below and its outstretched suburbs, to what must be Cape Point sticking out into the expanse of blue water. Only the sight wasn't quite as intoxicating as before. Not knowing Jace hung from a rope down a sheer rock face.

Thinking of him somewhere below made her legs wobble.

"Let's get you set up," the guide said.

"Let's not."

He laughed and put her into a harness anyway, instructing her on how to make the abseil. Okay, the rappel didn't sound too difficult, but talking and doing were totally different.

She looked at the camera. "I'm not sure about this."

"The harness will attach to a rope like this."

"The rope looks too narrow given what we ate in Buenos Aires."

"Don't worry. It's quite strong."

The minutes ticked by.

"Your teammate is doing fantastic," the guide said. "He's almost at the bottom."

"Great," she said. "Or not so great depending on your perspective."

"Millie."

She turned toward the sound of her name. Karen, wife of Lou, waved at her.

Oh, no. The red team had caught up with them.

"Your turn," the guide said.

Millie forced herself to breathe. She thought about the students at her school. She had to do this for them. That was the only way she could continue in the race and hope to win.

He attached her harness to the rope. Her only consolation was Jace had arrived at the bottom safely.

"I know you're frightened, but it's only one hundred and twelve meters down."

She did a quick mental calculation. Oh, boy. A little over three hundred and sixty feet. If she fell…

"You can do this," the guide continued.

He sounded just like Jace. "Did my teammate tell you to say that?"

"He did." The guide smiled. "Nice chap."

"He is."

Standing on the edge of the cliff, Millie thought about Jace's determination to get out of the trailer park. That had to be more difficult than abseiling down this, um, mountain.

Karen and Lou pulled on their gloves. One of them would start soon. That meant Millie had to go. Now.

Still she hesitated.

An image of the cowardly lion from *The Wizard of Oz* appeared in her mind.

You're one of the bravest people I know.

Jace was right.

She could be brave. Courageous.

Nothing was stopping Millie from doing this, but herself.

If they wanted the clue, if they wanted to win the million dollars, she had to do this. Even if the task killed her.

Heart pounding, she ignored her trembling legs and took the first step down. She looked up at her guide.

"You control the descent." He stood on the edge. "You won't go anywhere unless you want to. You don't need to hold on. Let go."

No way.

"Let me see your hands," he said.

With a deep breath, she let go. The rope attached to her harness held her in place. She didn't move.

"See." The guide grinned. "Now go."

Millie continued down, walking backward. Slowly. Carefully. The descent actually felt controlled. Soon the top seemed nonexistent. The noise faded. So did the rock she'd been walking down. She hung over Cape Town held only by a rope.

Don't think. Just do it.

She lowered herself down with the rope. Down, down, she went. Scary, yes, but fun, too.

"You're doing great, Freckles."

Jace. The sound of his voice filled her with relief.

Wanting to see him safe and sound, she glanced down.

White foam sprayed from the waves crashing over the rocks below. If the rocks didn't kill her, the pounding water would. She gulped.

"Don't look down," he said. "Just keep going."

"I can't."

"Come on. You can do it."

Jace continued to encourage her until she could finally descend again. She reached a point where gravity seemed to take over and soon she reached the bottom. A person handed her a clue pouch.

Satisfaction filled her. She'd made it.

"Good job, Freckles." Jace wrapped his arms around her, squashing the clue bag between them. "I know that was hard for you. I'm so proud of you."

Millie was proud, too, but all she wanted to do was sink into Jace's hug. Having his arms around her felt so good. Too good.

She backed out of his embrace. "The red team is right behind us."

"Lou's halfway down."

She took off the harness. "Let's get out of here."

"Thanks."

Millie might have told herself she'd done the abseil for her students, but that wasn't really true. She'd done it for Jace. She hadn't wanted to let him down, and she hadn't.

"You're welcome," she said. "But I couldn't have made it down without you."

Jace didn't know what he would have done without Millie. She showed a map to an older man on a bike to see if he knew where to catch the boat to Robben Island.

She laughed, the friendly sound lingering in the air and

complementing the music of a street musician at the Victoria and Alfred Waterfront, a dock with restaurants, shops and galleries.

The smiling man pointed at the map. No doubt Millie's easygoing manner had put him at ease. The way she'd done time after time asking people for directions. Amazing.

Intelligent, strong, easygoing, friendly and beautiful, too.

He couldn't ask for anything more in a woman. Teammate, he corrected, but each day he spent with Millie made his growing feelings for her harder to ignore.

Not feelings, he amended. Attraction.

Who wouldn't be physically attracted to such an incredibly gorgeous woman?

That's all he felt for her.

Well, that and respect.

Who wouldn't admire a woman who could overcome her fears every single day?

Looking around, the paradox of this beautiful place and the level of poverty he'd seen earlier in one of the townships struck him. Guilt crept down his spine. He never thought he had enough. He always wanted more, but these people had so little.

In some cases, almost nothing.

One of the street peddlers, a young boy selling painted flowers, caught Jace's attention. The boy's clothes were dark, like his skin. His pants too short. His jacket too big. He held a bucket full of ornamental flowers made out of some sort of metal—tin, perhaps—and painted bright colors.

He offered a flower to everyone who passed by him. No one had said yes yet, but the boy hadn't given up. If anything, he tried harder.

Jace watched him.

The hunger in the child's eyes probably matched the hunger in his belly. Just like the boy in Guatemala Millie had given money to. Just like Jace twenty years ago.

He found himself moving toward the boy.

"Flower, mister," the child said.

"How much?"

The boy raised his chin. "How much you give me?"

Jace gave him money leftover from this morning's tasks.

The boy's big eyes grew wider. "Sold, mister."

Jace regretted not having more to give him.

Grinning, the boy handed him a flower. "Dankie."

As the boy went to his next customer, Jace walked back to Millie. He gave her the flower.

Her eyes glistened. "Thank you."

He shrugged, uncomfortable with the emotion shining in her eyes. "It's just a flower."

"I'm not talking about the flower."

Jace shifted from foot to foot. "Did you get directions?"

"Don't change the subject. What you just did—"

"Anyone would do the same."

"No, they wouldn't."

She stared at him as if she could see right through him. Jace didn't like that. He felt exposed, vulnerable. He rocked back on his heels. Anything to put distance between them. "You might not look so happy when you find out I gave him a bunch of our money."

A light shone from her eyes as a grin broke out. "I don't mind."

And he knew she wouldn't. Another woman might, but not Millie. She would rather go hungry than let a child skip a meal. Look how far she was willing to go for her students. Not many teachers would do that.

"Jace—"

"I didn't do anything," he explained, feeling like a fraud. "He just reminded me of someone I used to know."

She looked at him for a long moment. "You."

"Let's go find our next clue."

The clue on Robben Island told them to drive thirty minutes to a winery in Stellenbosch. A check-in point or another delay, Millie had no idea.

As Jace drove on the wrong side of the road through the rolling hills covered with grapevines, she held the flower he'd given her. Even though it was made of tin, no flower smelled sweeter. She wanted to add the flower to the report card from her students so she could keep all her mementos together.

The car drifted to the right hand side of the road.

"Drive on the left," Millie reminded.

"Thanks, Freckles." He glanced back. "Next time you drive."

Warmth settled in the center of her chest. "Okay."

She'd learned so much about him in the past twenty-four hours. More of the puzzle pieces seem to be falling into place. She still wasn't finished, but she felt...closer.

Jace pulled to a stop in front of a winery and scrambled out of the car. "There's the clue box."

Millie climbed out of the back seat. Ryan followed her.

She grabbed a pouch from the box and unzipped it. A delay card was tucked inside. "Welcome to Stellenbosch. South Africa is the eighth largest producer of wines in the world. Over one billion liters are produced annually. You will help a vintner with his harvest. Each team must stomp enough grapes to fill a case of wine bottles to earn the next clue. Good luck!"

Millie removed her socks and shoes. She washed her legs and feet and climbed into a large half barrel. The grapes squished under her feet. She smelled a sweet scent.

Jace joined her. "This isn't so bad."

She raised her knees higher as she marched. Purple stained her feet and toenails. "I feel like I'm at a winery in Tuscany."

"Have you been to Tuscany?" he asked.

"Not yet, but I'd like to go."

"Ciao, bella."

"Grazie," she replied.

"Buongiorno."

She tried to think of a word. *"Arrivederci."*

"That's all I know," Jace admitted.

"Me, too. Unless we start naming pasta dishes and gelato flavors."

He raised a brow. "Gelato, huh?"

"My favorite."

"So what's your favorite flavor?" he asked.

You. "Um, Bacio."

"What's that?"

"Chocolate hazelnut," she said. "I also like *stracciatella.*"

"What?"

"Chocolate chip."

"And here I thought you were so versed in official Italian gelato." Jace tossed a grape at her.

"Be careful," she teased. "We might need that one."

He smiled. So did she.

It felt good to lighten up and have fun. They were no longer role playing, but she kept seeing new sides to him.

Millie had realized he wasn't Prince Charming. He wasn't Rico Suave. Nor was he the heartless groom. Jace Westfall was simply a man doing his best to put his past behind him.

The red team arrived. Suddenly the race was on and the red team was catching up fast.

"How many is that?" Millie asked.

"Eleven."

"One more to go."

"Done," Lou shouted as Karen hopped out of the barrel.

"Damn," Jace said.

Millie touched his forearm. "We're almost there."

A minute later, the vintner filled the last blue bottle and handed Jace a clue pouch. He ripped it apart. "Check-in."

Grape juice dripped their legs. They toweled off their purple feet, slipped on their socks and shoes and left their packs. Lou and Karen ran hard, but when the path angled abruptly up hill, Jace and Millie passed them. Running side by side, they increased the distance between the red team.

Adrenaline surged.

"We did it!" Excitement filled his voice.

Millie felt like skipping. "Told you so."

"You did." Jace hit the mat first. "Yes!"

She stopped herself by grabbing onto him. He took hold of her hand and laced his fingers with hers.

"Millie and Jace." Colt didn't hide a smile this time. "You are the first team to arrive. You win thirty thousand dollars."

Jace picked Millie up and spun her around. She giggled. He placed her on the ground, and the two of them faced Colt.

She bounced from foot to foot. She couldn't believe they'd won another leg and more money. She had twenty-five thousand dollars for her school. And Jace… He shot her a quick grin.

Jace had won twenty-five thousand for his business and his family. Not bad for the boy from the trailer park.

"You will have a twelve-hour layover here," Colt said. "So rest up."

Jace nodded. "We will."

Millie's mind continued to race. "I've figured the layover all out. Ten minutes to shower. Twenty minutes to eat. And eleven and a half hours to sleep."

"Sleep, huh?"

She nodded. "I've been dreaming of a full night's sleep since we left San Francisco."

"Do you plan to sleep alone?" Jace asked in a heavily accented voice.

She laughed. "I thought we left Rico Suave back in Buenos Aires."

"Does that mean Evita is never going to make another appearance?"

Millie stared down her nose at him. "Never say never."

Because she wouldn't mind doing another tango with Jace or even kissing him again.

CHAPTER EIGHT

KNEELING on the floor of a cabana on a white sand beach on Mahé Island in Seychelles located in the Indian Ocean, Millie dug through her backpack. She tried not to let nerves overwhelm her or look at the blue bikini she'd pulled out two minutes earlier. Maybe a production assistant had taken pity when stuffing Millie's backpack full of the blue clothing the show provided and tossed in a one-piece, too. "Please be in here."

The race had been going so well. She and Jace had been working flawlessly together since South Africa. They'd remained at the top of the pack.

The team to beat.

She couldn't be more pleased, except now they would be separated, in order to complete their solo stoppage challenges. Her task? Photograph six specific types of fish while snorkeling. Which is why she needed to find a one-piece. The teeny, tiny blue bikini wasn't going to work.

"Are you almost ready?" Jace asked from outside.

Of course, he was ready. He didn't need any special clothing to go fishing, but he didn't sound impatient. At least not yet. She glanced at the bikini. "Almost ready."

If only she'd chosen the solo stoppage task called

"bottom" instead of "top," then she would be the one bottom fishing and swimwear wouldn't be an issue.

"Hurry," Jace called from outside.

"Give me another minute." Millie could easily make up that amount of time. She searched the inner zipped pockets. She couldn't imagine the show packing only bikinis for the female contestants, especially the orange grannies.

Connie.

Millie's heart tightened. The orange team had been "canceled" after Ava refused to stomp grapes leaving Connie to do the task on her own. They'd been passed by two teams, the black and green, and sent home.

If she didn't hurry, Millie realized, the blue team would be next. She picked up the swimsuit.

Okay, she never wore a bikini. Not on *The Groom*. Not even as a teenager.

Modest? Yes? But mostly she was afraid of being inadequate somehow. Too flat. Too fat. And now…

"The black team is here."

Millie heard the impatience in his Jace's voice. She couldn't wait any longer.

She stripped out of her shorts, T-shirt and undergarments, hopping around on one foot. Wearing the bikini couldn't be as scary as abseiling or as frustrating as leading an ox-cart on the picturesque island of La Digue. She sprayed on sunscreen.

And if Jace made fun of her…

She gritted her teeth.

He wouldn't make fun of her. He'd liked Evita's plunging neckline and the thigh-high slit in her skirt, hadn't he? He'd like this.

She hoped.

Millie tugged the bikini bottoms up over her hips and tied the top. She took a sharp breath. The small pieces of blue fabric didn't cover much. *Don't think about it.* "Here goes nothing."

"Freckles?" he called out.

She ran out of the cabana with her water socks in her hand. "I'm right here."

Jace, wearing a pair of blue shorts and matching T-shirt, stood with whiter-than-white sand beach under his water sandals, swaying palm trees to his right and crystal-blue water to his left. A breeze rustled the palm fronds. She couldn't imagine a more picturesque, a more perfect sight.

Millie inhaled deeply, filling her lungs with the sea air.

But Jace wasn't admiring the beautiful scenery. He was staring at her. So was Ryan. Even Zack seemed to be looking around the camera eyepiece at her.

The appreciative gleam in their eyes made her shrink then stand taller. Maybe wearing the bikini had been a good idea after all.

Jace cleared his throat. His gaze lingered, practically caressed.

A slow heat burned its way through her. She'd never felt so desirable in her life. "Ready?"

"For what?"

"Hitting the bottom," she reminded. "I'm ready to be on top."

"So am I, babe." Derek clapped his hands together as he walked out of the other cabana in black swim trunks with Matt, in black shorts and a T-shirt, at his heels. "Damn, Millie you look hot."

Matt whistled. "Totally hot."

Hot. Millie wiggled her toes in the warm sand. She kind of liked being called that.

"Jackasses," Jace muttered.

She knew he was only looking out for her, the way he did with his mom and sisters. But Millie didn't want to be yet another responsibility to him. He didn't need that.

"They're harmless. Anyway, I can take care of myself."

Especially with these two. Derek was a dude, and Matt was a cutie. Outrageous flirts, yes, but their over-the-top compliments and silly innuendos boosted her confidence. "I have these two under control."

"Hear that, groom dude? Under control." Derek leaned back to get a peek at her backside. "Damn, Millie. I knew you had a nice bod, but not one so…sweet."

She laughed. "I'm going to miss you when this is over."

Jace's jaw set. "If we don't get going the race will be over sooner than we'd like."

Millie flushed. "Right. Let's go."

As they jogged over to the snorkeling and fishing guides, Millie was conscious of the bikini providing precious little support and coverage.

The fishing guide led Jace away.

With a wave, she hurried to the snorkeling site as Derek fell in step with her.

"You chose top? Hey, I chose top, too," he said. "I've started relationships with less in common."

"Do those kind of lines ever work?" she asked.

He grinned. "You'd be surprised."

Millie could imagine women falling for his easygoing charm. Just not her.

A phone rang. Only once, but the sound was so strange to hear while on a deserted beach. Or nearly deserted. She glanced back. The camera crews and production assistants crowded around.

"Wonder what's up?" Derek asked.

"All I know is I plan on finishing before you."

She sprinted ahead, kicking up sand as she ran.

Derek chased after her. "Damn, the groom dude is one lucky guy."

He could have ruined everything today.

That evening Jace stood on the veranda of the hotel in Seychelles with a drink in hand. The show was throwing the contestants a party later, but right now he enjoyed a rare moment of solitude.

The temperature had cooled slightly, but was still comfortable. A far cry from the temperatures on that South American glacier. But if Jace had his choice, he'd rather be back there where they'd had success, than here where they'd—he'd—almost let them lose.

Below him waves rolled to shore. Insects buzzed. Birds cawed. A perfect tropical setting. Setting was the right word. The Colonial-style architecture of the hotel looked more like a movie set than a place to spend the night.

Jace wasn't sure what was real or not anymore. He leaned against the railing.

"Did you hear?" Millie asked from behind him. "The camera crews get the night off. Do you know what that means?"

Feeling guilty, he didn't look back at her. "We won't have to smile at the party?"

"Exactly."

"That's great," he said. "Did you say goodbye to Karen and Lou."

"Yes." Millie joined him at the railing. "They weren't too surprised finishing last."

It could have been them.

Jace forced himself to look at her. He wasn't disappointed. The sexy off-the-shoulder style and above the knee hem of her blue cocktail dress surprised him. She never wore dresses like that during *The Groom*. Then again, he'd never seen her in a swimsuit until today, either.

He'd liked her in a bikini. "They ran a good race."

The ends of Millie's wavy hair bounced with each nod of her head. Her eyes were clear and bright. "I think they're going to make it. Their marriage, I mean."

"Good for them."

At least the race had saved a marriage. That had to count for something. He took a sip from his drink.

"Is everything going to be okay?" Concern filled her voice. "I mean, with your business and everything?"

Jace knew she would ask. He'd seen the questions in her eyes when they'd met up right before the check-in for this leg of the race. A quick rundown about the call from his sister about his business problem had been met with nothing but understanding. Still she deserved to know more. Everything.

But that didn't make telling her any easier.

Taking another drink, he watched a bird soar over the Indian ocean, swoop down and snag dinner. He felt like the fish with talons dug into its skin. Might as well get this over with.

"Yes." Jace had managed to put out a major fire thanks to his sister's emergency call today. Hell, he'd kept his largest client from taking his assets and going elsewhere. But taking the call had delayed him from getting on the fishing boat, putting the race at risk for him and Millie. "I'm sorry, Freckles."

"There's no reason to apologize."

"We could have been eliminated."

"We finished fourth."

"Out of five teams," he said, feeling like a useless jerk. "You finished your task first and had to wait there. For hours. Not knowing what had happened on my end."

She shrugged a bare shoulder. Her soft, smooth skin seemed to shimmer in the moonlight. "I was relieved nothing bad had happened to you."

"That might have made this easier to deal with."

"Don't say that. Your family needed you, Jace," Millie said. "I respect how you kept your priorities straight in the middle of all this. That's not an easy thing to do."

How could she make him feel so good when moments ago he'd felt like a complete loser?

Millie had become the one constant he could rely on. Not once had she let him down. She always gave her total support and understanding. He felt humbled and grateful. "Thank you."

"You'd do the same for me."

Jace hoped so, not wanting to let her down. Disappoint her. Again.

He stared at the moon, its crescent shape identical to the lagoon below.

"No matter what happens, don't forget we've won fifty thousand dollars," she said. "That's nothing to hang our heads about."

No kidding.

Teaming with Millie had shown Jace he'd never really known the real her. On *The Groom,* he'd only seen a quiet woman who made him feel comfortable in his role as pro-tector and caretaker. He hadn't realized she had her own strengths. During this race, she had not only pulled her own weight, but had taken care of him and challenged him, too.

He stared at her. Proud. "You're amazing."

Millie's confidence sparkled in her green eyes. She practically glowed, and he found her…irresistible.

"You're staring," she said.

"I can't help myself, Freckles."

She twirled around. "You like the dress."

"Yes, but that's not why I was staring." He set his drink on a nearby table. "You are the sexiest woman I've ever known, Millie Kincaid."

"That's not true, Desiree—"

"Knew she was sexy," he finished for Millie. "And that kind of confidence…well, it's attractive. But you—"

"Aren't that confident."

"You're not conceited," he corrected her. "And that is very, very sexy."

"Thank you," she said softly.

Her silhouette against the tropical setting took his breath away.

"No, thank you." He leaned toward her and brushed his lips over hers. A taste was all he wanted.

And he got it.

Sweet, warm, Millie.

Completely intoxicating.

Utterly addicting.

Jace knew one taste would never be enough.

He kept his lips against hers and kissed her again. Her scent—a mix of citrus and sunscreen—surrounded him. No way could he stop now. He didn't care.

Oh, he'd probably care later, but now he only had one thought on his mind.

Millie.

And more kisses.

Was that more than one thing?

He wrapped his hands around her, deepening the kiss. She willingly followed, matching kiss with kiss, and leaning into him until she couldn't move any closer.

His hands splayed the smooth skin on her back. Her breasts pressed against his chest. Blood rushed through his veins.

He wanted more of her. Hell, he wanted all of her.

Hunger took over, but Millie didn't seem to mind. Her lips eagerly moved over his, taking all he had to offer, giving all she could.

Millie leaned her head back. Jace accepted her invitation and left a trail of kisses up and down her neck. He nibbled on her earlobe.

She moaned. The sensual sound pushed him to the edge. Common sense told Jace to stop, but Millie apparently hadn't heard. Or seemed to care if she had. Her lips pressed against his. Searching, seeking, finding...

The same as him.

Except Jace now knew what he'd found...

Paradise.

And paradise had nothing to do with the white sand beaches, the blue-green waters, rustling palm trees and the sliver of moon hanging over the star-filled sky, but everything to do with the woman he kissed.

He'd felt incomplete his entire life, but with Millie in his arms, with her lips against his, he felt...whole.

That scared him. Hell, it terrified him.

Jace dragged his lips from hers.

"Wow," she said.

Wow was right. And that was very bad.

This wasn't Evita he'd kissed back in the tango bar. This was Millie standing here in this tropical Shangri-la. Sweet, capable, sexy Millie who stared at him with eyes full of emotion, eyes full of desire, eyes full of hope.

His chest tightened. What had he done now? Jace sucked in a breath. And how in the world was he going to fix it?

Where was he going?

As Millie stared at Jace's back walking toward the door, she tried to steady her uneven breaths, calm her speeding pulse. "Don't run away."

He stopped, turned. "I'm not running away."

"Then where are you going?"

A beat passed. "The party's starting."

"Who cares about the party?" Millie sure didn't. Not when her lips throbbed and her insides still quivered from his kiss. "We need to talk."

A muscle flicked at his jaw. He didn't want to talk, but she couldn't let him get away that easily.

Too much was at stake. And not just the race.

"Just for a minute. Please," she added.

He nodded once.

Uncertainty washed over her. Millie knew what she'd felt and she didn't want to lose that.

In his kiss she found the acceptance she'd been searching for all her life. In his arms she found the security she hadn't known she'd been seeking. In his life…

No, she couldn't get ahead of herself.

She wet her lips. "What just happened—"

"Was a mistake." His chin was set. His tone determined. His eyes dark. "I'm sorry."

Jace didn't want her. Old insecurities threatened to overwhelm her until she thought about their kiss.

He hadn't kissed her like a man who had no feelings for her. If anything, his kiss told her he cared about her.

So what was going on with this hot-and-cold routine?

She needed to find out before this affected not only the two of them, but their outcome on the race.

"Sorry?" For giving her a taste of Heaven or calling the kiss a mistake? Or both? Millie tilted her chin. "For what?"

He pressed his lips together.

"If you want to take your time to answer, that's fine." She sat on one of the comfortable chairs, sunk into the plush pillows and stared at the lagoon below. "I'm not in any rush."

He started to speak then stopped himself.

Millie felt his gaze on her, but she wasn't about to look his way. She couldn't waver. This wasn't only about the kiss or the race. This was about her. The way she'd kept up with him during the race and held her own and kissed him back. More was at stake than the million dollars.

"Sorry for kissing you," he said finally.

She studied him. "You didn't like it?"

He flinched. Surprised? She hoped so.

"Or did you like the kiss too much?" Millie continued.

His jaw tensed. "We're trying to win a million dollars. We need to concentrate on the race."

"Kisses would be too distracting."

"Hell, yes."

His words pleased her. Flattered her, too.

Okay, this she could deal with. She couldn't deny he made a good point.

"Kisses would be distractions," she admitted. "We've got a strong team."

"We don't want to jeopardize that."

"And risk losing the million dollars," she added. "Your family needs it."

"And your students."

But that wasn't all. At least not for Millie.

Her feelings for Jace were more grounded this time due to what they'd experienced and achieved together during the race. She'd gotten to know him better, seeing past his perfect, charming image to the real man underneath, a man she wanted to know better.

Fear of embarrassment wasn't holding her back, she realized. Fear of not having her feelings returned was. She couldn't forget what had happened the first time around. Jace wanted to win at any cost. He'd never tried to hide that.

What if this was just a way to keep their team together?

Even if it wasn't, a reality television show wasn't the place for a relationship to bloom. "Getting together in front of a television audience probably wouldn't be a good idea, either."

"That would be a bad idea."

"So we agree?" she asked. "No more kisses."

"No more kisses during the race."

Interesting wording. During the race. Millie hoped that meant more kisses after the race. Anticipation burst through her. A lot more kisses.

CHAPTER NINE

JACE didn't have to kiss Millie.

In fact, it was easy not to kiss her. The party at the hotel was too loud. Too public.

The plane ride from Seychelles to Rome was too long with Zack pointing his damn camera over the back of his seat at them. Even during takeoff and landing.

Ditto the train ride from Rome to Milan. So, okay, maybe Jace had spent a minute—or two or twenty—watching Millie sleep, her dark lashes in stark contrast to her pale face and light freckles, her hand curled under her cheek, but he hadn't thought about kissing her. Not that much anyway.

And who had time for kissing when they were solving a puzzle challenge at *Il Duomo di Milano* or hunting clues among the bustling shops of the *Via Montenapoleone?*

No, he didn't need to kiss Millie.

He wasn't going to kiss her.

Except now, watching her drive a race car around the track at *Autodromo Nazionale di Monza,* he couldn't think about anything else.

It was the car, he told himself. Hot, tight, fast. Any guy would fantasize watching a Ferrari being put through its paces and roaring by him only yards away.

It was the track. What red-blooded man's heart wouldn't skip a beat at the home of the Formula One Italian Grand Prix? The park setting with big trees shading the infield. The smell of oil and fuel, burning rubber and exhaust fumes perfuming the air.

It was...

"Woo-ee!" Derek whooped. "Look at that sweet thing handle that car."

Jace looked. Millie thundered through the *curva parabolica,* a long one-hundred-and-eighty-degree corner, and poured on the speed through the main straightaway.

Who was he kidding?

It was Millie. Her confidence. Her competence. Her joy.

Well, and the way she looked in her formfitting race suit.

He watched her drive a perfect line through the *chicane,* a serpentine curve.

Pride filled him. He only hoped this task and everything else she'd accomplished during the race would finally make her father take a long hard look at his courageous daughter.

"Go, Freckles," Jace shouted.

At this rate, they would have the fastest qualifying time of the four teams. The fastest team won the right to stand on the podium that protruded over the pit lane and straightaway and receive the first clue pouch. But Jace knew this was as much for Millie as it was about setting a fast time.

Derek leaned forward. "Damn, that girl is good."

She was good—in her heart, in her soul. She was one of the truly nicest people Jace knew. And she could drive.

"She's just getting started," Jace said.

"That's as fast as the instructor sitting next to you will let you go." Matt, who'd driven first, still wore his black driver's suit, but had pulled the top portion down and tied the sleeves around his waist. The teams were stuck at the track until all four teams posted a qualifying time to determine the order the clues would be handed out. "Any faster, you'll go off the track or into the wall."

Hitting the wall. Spinning off into the infield. Jace's gut tightened at the thought of something happening to Millie.

Hold it together, Freckles.

"Why aren't you driving, Jace?" Matt asked, challenge in his voice.

"It wouldn't have been fair if I drove."

Matt sneered. "Yeah, right."

"You've raced before, groom dude?" Derek asked.

Jace nodded. "Ever heard of SCCA Solo or autocross?"

Realization dawned on Matt's face. "Seriously?"

He nodded again.

"Man," Matt said. "It must be killing you not to be out there."

It was, but this had been Millie's turn to drive. Jace might have wanted the chance, but he wasn't about to take the opportunity away from her.

Together they'd made it this far. Together they would finish the race.

"She's hauling," Derek said.

Matt jabbed his teammate in the arm. "Not as fast as me."

"She's faster, dude," Derek said.

Jace nodded. "A lot faster."

Derek laughed. "Your girl is going to beat you, Matt-o."

His girl? As the muscles in Jace's shoulders tensed, his gaze darted between the two other men.

"She's not beating my time," Matt said, sounding more like a young kid than a twenty-something man. "And she's not mine...yet."

He slapped hands with Derek in a high-five gesture. Juvenile morons.

Jace gritted his teeth. "You might want to knock off the gestures, pal. You haven't scored."

And he wasn't going to, either, damn it. Not with sweet Millie.

His Millie.

Matt glanced at Jace. "She said you guys were just friends. I figured the door was open."

Time to slam it shut.

"We are friends," Jace said. "Close friends since the race started."

Matt motioned to Derek. "Us, too."

"You know it, dude," Derek said. "In a totally I-may-have-to-sleep-with-you-but-no-funny-stuff way, I mean."

"Totally."

Jace thought again of the way Millie had looked sleeping on the train and smiled.

"So how close have you and Millie gotten?" Matt asked suspiciously.

"Like you said…no funny stuff."

"Whoa," Derek said. "You haven't slept with her yet?"

Jace wanted to discourage Matt, but Millie would never forgive him if he implied they were having sex on national television. "Millie's a great teammate. Under different circumstances, I'd love to take it to the next level. But—"

"But what?" Matt leaned forward. "Spill, man."

Jace hesitated. What could he say to keep Matt away?

"Millie Kincaid is high maintenance," Jace said finally. "Not in the money way. But she expects a lot from a relationship. Millie's a forever kind of girl. Not the fling type."

Which is what made her so special, Jace realized.

Derek snickered and elbowed Matt. "Told you so."

"What makes you think I'm looking for a fling?" Matt asked.

"Because you're a paramedic," Derek said. "A fireman. Chicks dig that. Why settle for one when you could have many?"

"Exactly," Jace said, not believing he agreed with Derek on something. "Millie won't settle for being anything but a man's number one."

She deserved no less. Which was why it would be impossible to give Millie what she needed. The realization left him feeling...unsettled.

Derek shivered. "Scary."

"Very." Jace's feelings about her confused him more than they had during *The Groom*. "Millie loves her job and the small town where she lives. She won't leave her comfort zone."

The words coming out of his mouth sounded so wrong. All Millie had done since they started the race was step out of her comfort zone.

"I think you're wrong, man. That doesn't sound like the Millie I know," Matt said.

It didn't sound like the woman Jace knew, either.

Damn, he had pigeonholed her. During *The Groom* and *Cash Around the Globe*. Sweet, unworldly, small town Millie. He had no idea what she was like at home or what home meant to her or what home looked like.

He hadn't wanted to know.

Thinking of Millie so simplistically had made it easier for Jace to walk away from her. To pretend he was doing the right thing for her, when really he was only protecting himself.

"I'm still going for it," Matt said, sounding determined.

"Millie wants the entire package." Jace figured Millie's dream would dead bolt the door on the paramedic. "A devoted husband, a minivan in the driveway of a house with a picket fence, a couple kids and—"

"A dog. A chocolate lab named Hershey. She told me," Matt finished for him. "Me, too."

This guy knew what she wanted to name her dog? Jace hadn't known that. He shifted his weight to the other foot.

Not good.

Especially when Matt had more to offer Millie. A steady paycheck and benefits. No struggling business to save. No needy family to care for.

As Jace stared at the blue car racing around the track, a weight pressed down on his chest. Matt could give Millie all the things she wanted. All the things she deserved.

"Don't get ahead of yourself, dude," Derek said. "You haven't even been alone together."

"I've seen enough during the race to know she's perfect for me," Matt said.

Okay, thanks to the words "race" and "perfect," everything made sense to Jace.

"Don't get swept up in the fantasy of reality television, Matt," Jace cautioned. "Emotions are exaggerated. People seem different. But once the cameras stop rolling, real life crashes down on you."

"Listen to the groom dude, Matt-o," Derek said.

"Millie deserves a happily ever after." Jace watched the blue car pull to a stop. "You have to ask yourself if you can deliver one or not."

Matt's eyes brightened. "So that's why you chose Desiree."

It wasn't a question. Good thing because Jace didn't—couldn't—answer.

"I'd have chosen Desiree, too." Derek blew on the tips of his fingers. "She was hot."

Hot, yes. But she was also driven and ambitious. Desiree hadn't really been interested in a romantic relationship, not at the expense of her acting career.

Which meant—Jace winced—Desiree was just like him.

"Would you choose Desiree?" Matt asked. "Or Millie? If you had to choose over again."

Millie exited the car, a mixture of grace and athleticism. Her driving instructor helped her remove the blue helmet. Wet hair plastered to her head, she waved.

Desire hit him low and hard, but his feelings for Millie went deeper than physical attraction. She was smart, caring, funny, loyal. Everything about her from her freckles to her dedication to her students had endeared her to him. She wasn't perfect, but she was pretty damn close. His heart knew what choice to make...

Millie.

As his throat worked mechanically, he forced himself to breathe. Choosing Millie, then or now, would change everything and throw his life into a tailspin. Just the thought left Jace feeling as if he'd crashed into a wall going one hundred and eighty miles an hour.

He'd never walk away in one piece.

And that, he realized, was the bottom line.

With Millie he had no control over his heart, his emotions, his life. He'd known it from the beginning. Desiree had been a safer choice.

"Desiree's a better match," he answered.

Safer, not better.

Millie headed his way with a bounce to her step and a beaming smile on her face. "We're in first place."

"Great job." Jace fought the urge to pull her into his arms and shook her hand instead. Her skin was soft and smooth, but the action felt wrong and awkward and he couldn't wait to let go. "You're going to be hard to beat."

Her eyes sparkled. "Don't you mean we're going to be hard to beat?"

We.

"Yeah, sorry."

"The groom dude's sorry." Derek snickered. "But not as sorry as he'll be when Millie hears who he'd choose all over again."

"When I hear what?" she asked.

Jace clenched his teeth. "Shut up."

Matt hummed a tune.

"Isn't that the song 'Desiree' by Keith Urban?" Millie asked.

Derek laughed. "And with that we're out of here."

The two men walked away, leaving Jace with a confused looking Millie and an eager cameraman filming every word.

"So what's going on, Jace?" Her forehead creased. "And what does it have to do with Desiree?"

"Are you going to tell me?" Millie asked not caring Zack and Ryan stood right there. Who knew when she'd have Jace alone?

Jace looked at the car on the track being driven by Krystal from the purple team. "The guys asked me if I would choose Desiree if I had to do it all over again."

"And you said…"

"I said she was a better match for me."

"Oh." Millie didn't know what else to say. Not when everything she thought she knew about Jace, about their future together had suddenly blown up in a matter of seconds. "I thought you said choosing Desiree had been a mistake."

"Because I wasn't in love with her."

Good answer.

But not, unfortunately, the answer Millie was hoping for. Waiting for. She wanted to hear that Jace was in love with her, Millie. That not choosing her had been a mistake, one he wanted to rectify as soon as the race was over.

She would forgive him.

She'd already forgiven him.

But he didn't say a word.

He hadn't been able to express his real feelings back at the hotel when the cameras weren't rolling. She'd been content to wait then, on the promise of something more, but now she wasn't. She no longer thought of herself as quiet and anxious. She wanted to know the truth.

"So why would you say Desiree is the better match?" Millie asked, impatience getting the best of her.

"We have the same priorities and want the same things out of life."

"Baloney."

"Excuse me?"

"I don't believe you." Millie wasn't about to listen to this. "I watched *The Groom*. You never kissed Desiree the way you kiss me."

He flinched at the word kiss, and though Millie was sorry for saying it on camera, she needed to pin him down. "Okay, but—"

"You never talked to her the way you talk to me."

"True, but—"

"So stop the bull and tell me what's going on?"

Jace flinched. "What's gotten into you?"

You. "I want to know where I stand."

He smiled at her, warm and charming as ever. "After the way you drove, you're ready to stand on the winner's podium."

But this time Millie wasn't going to allow him to deflect her with a compliment and a joke.

She swallowed. "I'm not talking about the race. Has everything that's happened between us been part of the show or is something there?"

"You're not pulling your punches today."

"Answer my question, please. You kissed me. Are you going to say that didn't mean anything?"

"When I kissed you… Yeah, something was there when we kissed."

Thank goodness.

"And afterward…"

He hesitated.

She pressed. "Are you saying we're just getting caught up in the fantasy again? Is this happening because we've been thrown together in the race? Is this all an act or do we have something real we can build on?"

"Whether it's real or not…I have other commitments, Millie. To my work. To my family. I can't give you the life you want."

She let the words sink in.

"I like you, Freckles," he continued earnestly.

Like, not love.

A sense of déjà vu overcame her. Her heart was too numb to hurt.

"I really do," he continued. "But I'm not in a position to be a husband or father."

"Because of your business and family."

"Among other things," he said. "You deserve so much more than I can give you."

She listened to his words half-stunned, half-outraged.

"We're better off as only teammates," he added.

Tears stung her eyes, but she blinked them away. "You know what, Jace?"

"What?"

"You're right." She squared her shoulders. "We are better off as teammates."

"You're a wonderful person, Millie," Jace said, his expressive blue eyes sincere. "And a great competitor. You deserve to win."

He was breaking her heart.

"I deserve more than that. I deserve a man who isn't afraid to go after what he wants in life. Or me."

"Who's afraid?" Jace asked.

"Not me." Disappointed and humiliated and miserable, yes. But... "I'm not going to be afraid anymore."

"Teammates"? Millie thought miserably two days later.

"Great competitors"? Ha.

They'd managed to avoid fighting on camera. In fact, they barely spoke to one another at all. And their lack of communication, the tension seething just below the surface, was taking its toll. They'd been lucky to get out of Helsinki on the same flight as the other three teams.

"How much farther?" Jace asked as he drove from a reindeer farm outside Rovaniemi, the capital of Lapland in Northern Finland.

She checked the map again. "Three kilometers."

"I thought you said three kilometers two kilometers ago."

"I might have misread the map," she said. "Sorry."

"We can't afford to make any mistakes."

"I'm doing my best," Millie said, hoping to sound cheerful and not angry. Or exhausted. She crinkled the edge of the map. The show must have assumed since the sun never went below the horizon in the Arctic Circle in July the racers didn't need to sleep, but the so-called endless night was catching up to them. "Trying to figure out a map in a language I don't read when I haven't slept in twenty-four hours isn't easy."

He attempted a smile. "You should have tried reindeer lassoing."

"I had my hands full feeding the herd."

Millie yawned. The lack of sleep hadn't helped them get along any better. Italy hadn't been a check-in point, only a stop on the race to Finland. At least no sleep meant no dreams about Jace. She hated her subconscious betraying her resolve to put him out of her mind and heart once and for all.

He glanced back. "Do you want to take a nap?"

"No thanks," she said. "A check-in point has to be coming up after this stop unless they want the top three teams to fade during the finale."

"You're probably right," Jace said. "This Santa visit has everything to do with the December finale air date so I bet the layover will be in Lapland."

He was making an effort to talk to her. To recapture the easy communication they'd enjoyed before.

Before she'd practically begged him to tell her they had a future together and he'd told her he wanted to be friends.

Millie gripped her hands together in her lap. "Christmas in July?"

"Well, we're on our way to Santa's place." He didn't sound too happy about it, but he hadn't sounded happy since Monza. Neither of them had. "Let's just hope they don't stick us in red fat suits and ask us to play Santa."

Despite her misery, the prospect of Jace in costume made her smile. "Want to practice your ho, ho, hos just in case?"

Zack and Ryan nodded enthusiastically.

"No," Jace said. "But you can."

Ryan mouthed a heartfelt please.

Millie didn't want to, but she forced a smile at the camera anyway. "Ho, ho, ho."

"Weak," Jace said. "Very weak."

"At least I'm not afraid to try," she snapped.

He stared out the windshield.

The camera continued to roll.

Oops. She tried again. "Ho, ho, ho."

"Good job," Jace said, his voice sounding forced.

Zack gave her a thumbs-up sign. Ryan blew her a kiss. At least the film crew was happy. She sighed. "Santa's place is on the right."

He parked. Together, with Zack and Ryan, they entered a quaint looking facility making Christmas in July seem like a real possibility. An elf, complete with pointed hat, ears and shoes, led them into Santa's office. "The big man will be right with you."

A large wooden chair sat by a fireplace with a giant black pot hanging in front of it. The fire crackled and popped, making Millie think of cold winters back home in Oregon except she'd never felt so far away from home. Two benches flanked each side of the chair.

"Take a seat," the elf said then walked out, the bells on his shoes jingling.

Jace sat on the bench closest to the fireplace. Millie sat on the edge of the round table. A tense silence filled the air. Forget being teammates. They were more like strangers now.

"Ho, ho, ho." Santa wore a red vest over a white long-sleeved shirt, green pants and brown boots. Only his pointy red hat, rosy cheeks, wire-rimmed glasses and long white beard were similar to the Santa she'd known as a child. He sat between them. "It's never too early to start planning for Christmas. What would you like Santa to bring you?"

Jace raised his eyebrows. "How about a shiny new bike?"

Santa didn't smile at his joke. "Most men wouldn't be content with that."

"What do most people ask for?" Millie asked.

"Fame. Wealth. Love," Santa said.

"We've had enough fame," Jace muttered.

Santa's eyes were shrewd. "Then…wealth? Or love?"

Millie's heart constricted.

"Wealth, I guess," Jace said, as she knew he would. "Bring me a couple of decent financial statements for my business, and I'll handle the rest."

Santa pulled at his beard. "I'll see what I can do."

"Thanks," Jace said.

"And what would you like Santa to bring you this year?" Santa asked Millie.

Love.

But not the one-sided love she felt for Jace. She remembered what she'd said to him. *I deserve a man who isn't afraid to go after what he wants in life. Or me.*

"I would like," she lowered her voice slightly. "A happily ever after."

She heard Jace's sharp intake of air. Not surprising.

He'd made it perfectly clear that wasn't what he wanted from life. Or with her.

"Can you be a little more specific?" Santa asked.

Millie leaned toward him, his curly white beard tickling her chin, and whispered so only he could hear. "I want a husband who loves me, healthy children, a house of our own and a dog."

Santa's mouth quirked. "That's a tall order."

Millie sighed. "I know."

But she didn't want to settle for anything less.

"I'll do my best." Santa thought for a moment. "Anything else you want in case I run into problems?"

"How about the dog?" she suggested loud enough so Jace and the film crew could hear. "A puppy, that is."

"A chocolate lab puppy," Jace added. "Named Hershey."

"How did you know?" she asked him.

"Lucky guess."

It didn't matter. He didn't matter.

Santa's blue eyes twinkled. He released a booming ho-ho-ho. "I might be able to pull this off."

A puppy wouldn't be so bad. A puppy would keep her company. A puppy would love her back. "Thank you, Santa."

Santa smiled. "Be good and you'll get what you want."

Being good hadn't gotten her anywhere, Millie thought with an ache at her heart. At least, it hadn't gotten her Jace's love.

Be good and you'll get what you want.

Jace didn't know what he wanted anymore. Except to win.

And he was afraid he wasn't going to get that.

They'd lost their edge, their teamwork, everything.

Millie packed her backpack after the extended layover.

They'd been lucky to finish in third place. If not for the purple team taking a wrong turn, he and Millie would have been the team sent home.

"We need to regroup." The red light on the camera mocked him. "We could have been canceled."

"I know." She looked down. "I'm sorry. I've been a little…distracted. And upset ever since—"

"Monza."

She nodded.

"Me, too." He took a deep breath. "Want to start over?"

"Can we?"

"Yes." He wanted to go back to the way things had been. "It might be the only way to stay in the race."

"Okay, it's just…"

He didn't like the sound of her voice and leaned toward her. "What is it, Freckles?"

"I know I'm racing for my school, but I'm…I'm ready for this to be over with."

Jace had entered the race with one goal in mind. To win. His entire life had been consumed by taking care of his family. He'd strived to be successful for them, to make up for what his father had taken away from them—stability.

But now, thanks to Millie, he wondered if he was missing out on more of what life had to offer. Maybe he had been afraid. Maybe once he got things straightened out, when his business wasn't struggling and his family taken care of, he would have more to offer…someone.

"Have you thought about what happens if we don't win?" Millie asked.

Every single day. "I'm trying not to."

"Me, too, but today as we were heading to the check-in point. I thought we were going to be last." She zipped her pack. "I decided to come up with a contingency plan in case we, well, were sent home."

He admired her for thinking ahead. "Smart idea."

"I thought you would tell me to think positively."

"No. Tell me about your plan."

"I thought I could raise the money myself," she explained. "I've never been much for putting myself out there and asking for things, but after this race, I think I could do it."

"That's the spirit, Freckles."

"But I'd rather not," she admitted.

"You won't have to. We're going to win this thing."

She smiled at him. "Together."

Jace forced an answering smile. He had no other choice. "Together."

CHAPTER TEN

From Finland, they flew to Canada. Horseback riding in Calgary. White water rafting near Banff National Park. And now this...

Together they would either succeed or fail. Jace hadn't considered the latter option. Until now.

He reread the delay card. "Each team member must do a tandem skydive jump with a professional instructor in order to receive the next clue. Only one team per plane. If one or both members choose not to jump, the team will be assessed a three-hour penalty."

Millie tugged on a strand of hair. "There are so many other things we could do in Canada, you think they could come up with something more original than skydiving."

Her casual words might have masked her fear to anyone, but him. Millie was afraid of heights. Just because she'd abseiled didn't mean she was ready to skydive.

If one or both members choose not to jump...

A three-hour penalty would kill any chances they had of winning.

"What do you want to do?" he asked.

She stared up at the cloudless blue sky. "I want to get up in that plane before the other teams arrive."

His heart swelled with pride. "You're really something, you know that."

She sent him a trembling smile. "I told you I wasn't going to be afraid anymore, but..."

He took her hand and squeezed gently. "But what?"

"Let's get up there before I change my mind."

Jace knew how frightened she must be, but Millie wasn't showing one ounce of fear. He longed to kiss her. Hell, he wanted to hold her in his arms and never let go. He took her hand instead and gave squeezed gently. "Thank you."

"Don't thank me yet," she said. "I haven't jumped."

Jace knew she wouldn't let him down. He picked up his blue jumpsuit, helmet and goggles. "You will."

"Right." She picked up her equipment. "Even if I'm sure it's going to kill me."

"You won't die."

"How do you know?"

"The producers would never allow it to happen." Jace hoped to ease her concern with a joke. "Death sells, but they'd never be able to top those ratings next season."

"Gee, thanks."

He grinned. "That's what teammates are for."

Standing on an airplane at thirteen thousand feet somewhere above British Columbia, Canada, felt wrong on so many different levels. So did being strapped to an instructor named Thor. Millie didn't care how many successful jumps the guy had made. One bad jump would negate all the others. She squeezed her eyes closed.

Millie had no doubt. She was going to die.

Her life passed quickly before her eyes. Except for

teaching her students and being Jace's partner in this race, she had little to show for the past twenty-six years.

Talk about depressing.

At least she'd have an exciting obituary plus her death on film. How many people could say that? And her father couldn't call her a coward any longer.

Her instructor moved closer to the opening. A cameraman stood by the large hole. No way would she call that a door.

Millie wanted to go back to Jace, who stood behind them. He believed in her. He was proud of her. He wouldn't let anything happen to her. Fear lodged in her throat.

"Are you ready to skydive?" her instructor asked.

She could barely hear anything due to the plane's engine and wind. "I, uh."

You're really something.

She clung to Jace's words like a lifeline. Millie realized she was doing this as much for him as herself.

The instructor scooted forward. Her feet dangled from the plane. Before she could say stop or goodbye, they tumbled away hurling into nothingness.

Loud, cold, windy.

Millie screamed, clutching her harness as the air exerted pressure against her body. A couple of seconds later, they seemed to stabilize. Okay, they weren't exactly stable, but she felt like her instructor had more control, as if they were flying, not falling.

This portion of the free fall wasn't the plummeting to Earth, where-is-my-stomach amusement park ride sensation. This felt…different. Less scary. More exhilarating.

The air seemed to support her, almost holding her up. She wondered how Jace was doing and knew he'd love every minute of the ride down.

Millie felt a jolt. The parachute.

Suddenly she was floating under a canopy on a gentle ride down. She flashed the thumbs-up sign to a cameraman who had jumped at the same time.

The descent was amazingly peaceful. She enjoyed seeing the landscape below and gave a cheer when the instructor made loops and spins on the peaceful ride to the ground. The landing was softer than she could have imagined, smoother than the abseil landing at Table Mountain in Cape Town.

Zack and Ryan were waiting for her on the ground.

"Wow," she said to the camera.

Ryan and Zack did a mini version of the wave.

As soon as she was out of the harness, Millie watched Jace and his instructor make a perfect landing. She ran over to him.

"How did you do?" he asked, taking off his goggles and helmet.

She laughed. "I'm alive."

"So you liked it."

It wasn't a question. "I...yes. You?"

"I wish we could jump again." His smiled crinkled the corners of his eyes, and her heart went bump. "I loved skydiving."

If only he loved her.

"I know what you mean. I've never felt such a rush." She removed her goggles and helmet. "And now that I've done this, I know I can do anything myself."

Jace stared at her with a strange look in his eyes.

"What?" she asked.

"Come on," he said. "Let's get the clue."

Millie ran to the clue box, grabbed a clue pouch and opened it. "Welcome back to Earth."

No kidding. After the adrenaline rush she felt as if she'd been plopped headfirst back into the race.

She continued reading. "Take the path from the airport. Route flags will mark the direction you are to follow. Hurry. You never know what is waiting for you around the bend."

Jace frowned. "I don't like the sound of that."

She stepped out of the jumpsuit and put on her backpack. "Maybe the clue writers are just getting tired like us."

"Maybe."

After a half mile of running, Millie came to a bend. "This might be it."

He glanced backward. "I hope so. A team is right on our tail, but I don't know if it's black or green."

She ran faster, rounding the bend. Fifty yards away, Colt stood on a mat.

What was he doing here? Her pulse quickened.

"This can't be a check-in point," Jace said.

Millie had no idea but that didn't stop her from sprinting to the mat. Jace beat her by three steps. She bent over to catch her breath, and he held onto the top of her back until she stood upright.

"Jace and Millie," Colt deadpanned. "You are team number one."

"This is an official check-in point?" Jace asked.

"Yes," Colt answered. "We said there would be twists to the race."

But Millie hadn't been expecting this. She exchanged surprised looks with Jace. Okay, they'd managed to regroup and come in first, but what did that mean for the two teams behind them? And the remainder of the race?

"For finishing first on this leg of the race, your team has won sixty thousand dollars."

Millie covered her mouth with her hands. Jace looked as shocked as she felt. They had won one hundred and ten thousand dollars. That was fifty-five thousand each.

"I don't believe it," she said.

"Believe it." Jace picked her up and swung her around. After he placed her on the ground, he hugged her. He nuzzled against her neck, his warm breath was like a forbidden caress.

Heat pooled deep within her. Having him hold her shouldn't feel so good, shouldn't make her want to kiss him so badly.

"We need you to wait for the other teams to finish so we can go over a few things," Colt said.

Millie stepped out of his embrace, but not before he whispered in her ear. "Looks like another twist."

She nodded. Not that a new twist mattered much. The race was almost over. They'd won more prize money. She should be happy, but the moment felt bittersweet. Once they crossed the finish line, she wouldn't see Jace again.

Jace was suddenly reluctant to hear about the game twist. He didn't want the next leg to start because once the race was over, he and Millie would no longer be teammates. He would no longer have a reason to see her again.

"Listen up blue and black teams," Colt said. "The green team is out. You have a choice. You can vote to keep your same team or you can vote to disband your team and compete alone during the final leg of the race for the million dollars. The final vote affects both teams."

"What about the money we've won so far?" Millie, ever practical, asked.

"You still split whatever you won as a team," Pete said.

"One team member will keep the original film crew. The other will be assigned a new crew."

"Bummer," Derek said.

"One more thing, if you vote to split, there can be no alliances," Pete added. "You must work on your own or you will be disqualified. The final prize money cannot be split."

"More for me," Derek said.

Matt winced.

Colt handed each of them a piece of paper and a pen. "Write the word 'split' if you want to disband your team and compete separately. Write the word 'team' if you want to stay together until the end. Majority vote wins."

Millie scribbled on her paper. So did Derek and Matt. Jace stared at the blank page in his hand.

They'd vowed to win together. But together suddenly meant more than this race. Much more than teammates.

And that…scared him.

Jace had spent most of his life taking care of his family. He'd been the protector and the provider.

With Millie, it would be different. She was his equal. She'd conquered her final fear and jumped out of an airplane. She was the most amazing woman he'd ever known. He could end up hurting her, but she could just as easily hurt him.

I deserve more than that. I deserve a man who isn't afraid to go after what he wants in life. Or me.

He was desperately afraid she would never see him as that man. A man who loved her. A man who would be worthy of her.

What if she left him, the way his father had left him, his sisters and mother? Millie said she was eager for the race to be over. Didn't that mean in her heart she'd abandoned all thoughts of a future with him? What did she want?

I know I can do anything myself.

Millie didn't need him. She could take care of herself better than he could take care of her. Jace saw that now. And so had she.

He wrote a word and passed the paper to Colt.

Colt read the first one. "Splitso."

Derek smiled.

Colt opened the second one. "Split. That's two votes for splitting the teams."

"What if it's a tie?" Millie asked.

"Let's see what this third paper says first." Colt unfolded it. "Team."

Millie smiled confidently at Jace. His heart lodged his throat.

"And the final vote is for—" Colt held the paper in his hand for a long moment. "Split."

Derek and Matt pumped their fists and shouted. Jace stared at a disappointed Millie.

Her eyes glistened and she blinked. "You said we were going to finish together."

"I'm sorry."

"Sorry?" she asked. "Sorry doesn't cut it. We were supposed to be teammates."

"We are teammates."

"You mean, we were."

His act of self-preservation had exploded in his face.

"I thought you wanted..." He hadn't been thinking. He'd been too afraid. "I wasn't thinking straight."

"I knew you were only interested in winning." Her nostrils flared. "I just had no idea it meant everything to you."

She had it wrong. "Millie, please—"

"Save it, Jace," she said. "You're the last man on Earth I want to talk to right now."

Millie was too upset to touch the barbecue dinner provided that night.

"You need to eat, Freckles," Jace said, appearing before her with a loaded plate.

Her stomach lurched. She could barely look at him. Let alone eat. Teammates, he'd said, and she had believed him.

She was a fool.

"You're not my teammate so don't worry about what I eat." She rubbed her forehead. "Anyway, I can't think about food right now. Not with the game twist—"

"Don't think," he urged. "Just run your race."

"Is that what you plan to do?" she asked.

He nodded. "I doubt Derek and Matt are going to lose any sleep over this game twist, either."

But Millie didn't care about the black team. She cared about Jace. "How about you?"

"I'd rather we finished together, but that's not going to happen now."

"Not since your vote," she said bitterly.

"About that, Freckles." His lips pressed together. "I made a mistake."

"Your second one."

"That's not fair."

"Fair?" Her blood pressure spiraled. "Nothing about this has been fair. We were supposed to be teammates. I believed you when you said we'd finish together. I trusted you."

He looked down at his plate of food. "I said I was sorry."

"That's not good enough." And it wasn't. She deserved

better from him. "How many times are you going to let me down in front of the camera, Jace?"

"Never again."

"Those are just words." Tears stung her eyes. "After everything that's happened, how can I ever trust you again?"

CHAPTER ELEVEN

MILLIE had started the race on her own. She would end it on her own.

Not that she was really on her own. Her new film crew—she'd dubbed them Bert and Ernie—had joined her on the flight to Seattle. The two men followed her to Pike's Market where she tossed fish as the sun came up and to the famous coffee franchise where she made coffee for the early morning rush of customers. They were with her on a helicopter ride to the Mount Saint Helens Recreation Area and now sat in the car as she drove around the steam-spewing volcanic crater. The rules of the race prevented Bert and Ernie from helping her, of course, but Millie didn't need their assistance.

Or Jace's.

The car vibrated on the road. She gripped the steering wheel tighter.

She didn't need Mr. Just-run-your-race to read the map, to pillow her head against his strong shoulder or wink at her when the going got tough. To encourage her with a warm smile or quiet praise. No, she didn't need Jace Westfall.

But, oh, how she missed him.

At least he could never let her down again.

At the Norway Pass trailhead, Millie parked the car, turned off the ignition and reread the clue aloud for the sake of the camera. "On May 18, 1980, Mount Saint Helens erupted. A powerful explosion decimated hundreds of square miles of lush, beautiful landscape. You will hike the Boundary Trail from Norway Pass to the Johnston Ridge Observatory. The winner will be the first to cross the finish line at the lower observatory deck on Johnston Ridge. Good luck!"

Only one other car was parked in the parking lot for the trailhead. Second place. Her heart tripped faster. She still had a chance to win.

On her own.

She could show her students what you could achieve when you set your mind to something. She could show her father how wrong he'd been about her all these years.

But winning would be a hollow victory. All the prize money in the world wouldn't buy her the one thing she had longed for her entire life...unconditional love.

Millie put on a blue daypack provided by the show. Inside were water bottles, a blue hat, sunscreen, her memento—the report card from the students—and the tin flower Jace had given her in Cape Town. She headed to the trailhead.

The uphill climb wasn't too hard and provided beautiful views. The new growth pine trees, shrubs and colorful flowers surprised her. She'd expected to see a moonlike landscape, but didn't dare stop and enjoy the scenery.

The hike looked to be over ten miles long. The key to this final challenge, Millie realized, was pacing herself.

As she continued the hike, she pointed out a scurrying chipmunk to the camera and the steam coming from the crater only a few miles away. Sun-bleached downed trees and stumps dotted the hillside, new pine trees sprouting up among them.

Already Bert and Ernie seemed to be dragging. She sure missed Zack and Ryan.

But not nearly as much as she missed...

No, she wasn't going there again.

Millie focused on the trail, catching sight of Spirit Lake. One end was full of logs. Similar dead trees littered the mountainside, as if a child had tossed a can of pickup sticks everywhere. Large or small, the trees hadn't stood a chance against the powerful force of the eruption.

The trail followed the geography of the land, rising and falling. Mountain peaks appeared in the distance. Wooden signs marking the Boundary Trail and pointing to other paths, such as the Lake Trail and way back to Norway Pass, kept her going in the right direction.

As she traveled farther, the vegetation became sparse. She noticed more downed trees. Grayer dirt. A sense of desolation. The vast wasteland of volcanic destruction was more of what she expected. Each one of her steps sent a small cloud of ash-soil mixture into the air.

"Put one foot in front of the other and stay away from the edge."

Somewhere at the end of the trail lay Johnston Ridge Observatory and the finish line. The end. That's what she needed to focus on.

The hot July sun beat down. Millie's thighs burned. Her lungs protested. Her heart ached.

Because of exertion, she reminded herself. Not Jace.

Don't think about him.

They were no longer a team. They probably never had truly been one, but that couldn't change the way she felt about him.

Her overused muscles, her sore back would all heal. But her heart... She wasn't so sure. Her heart felt like the gray barren landscape surrounding her.

Jace had told her he wanted to be friends. He'd told her he wanted to be teammates.

And then he'd dumped her. Duped her. Again.

He'd chosen the chance to compete and win on his own rather than risk sharing the prize with her. He'd put his responsibility to his company and his family first. Millie could understand that. But just once in her life, she longed for someone to choose her.

To share her dreams.

To put her first.

Jace hadn't.

And he wouldn't.

The thought was a fresh cut to her already wounded heart. But someday her heart would heal, just as parts of the once-decimated landscape she'd passed through earlier on the trail showed signs of new life, growth, healing.

She glanced back. Only Bernie, the sound guy. No sign of another racer coming up behind her. Still she picked up the pace. She needed to pass whoever was in front of her.

Her right foot slid on the dirt. Small rocks tumbled over the side. The trail wasn't narrow, but the path bordered a steep drop-off. A cliff really. Panic ricocheted through her. Millie reached something to hold onto and grazed her palm on a large rock, but she righted herself.

Millie clenched her hand tight and breathed deep, trying to calm her staccato heart. She needed to focus. She'd have all the time she needed—all the rest of her life—to analyze the fiasco with Jace after she reached the finish line. Right now she needed to race.

Raising her chin, she glimpsed puffs of ash hanging in the air. Another racer was ahead of her. A runner in black. And his crew. Matt, tearing up the trail.

She was so tired, hot and sore.

You can do it, Freckles, she imagined Jace saying. *You're fast. Don't give up.*

She wanted him out of her head and out of her life, but his encouraging words helped.

Millie pushed harder, quickening her steps. Soon she could taste the dirt and ash lingering in the air from Matt and his crews' footsteps. That gave her the boost she needed. Just a little further... Faster.

Ahead of her, Matt stumbled, his running shoes scraping on gravel. Her heart caught in hope. And then in fear as Matt flung out his arms, fighting for balance. Dirt and ash and pebbles flew into the air. He grunted. His feet slid over the edge. She cried out, reaching toward him, but he was too far away. Rocks slid and crashed into each other.

And then he was gone.

Adrenaline shot through her veins. She sprinted to his camera crew. "Where is he?"

Matt's new camera guy panned the cliff. "I'm looking for him."

"Matt?" she yelled. "Matt? Where are you?"

No answer.

Sweating, she leaned over the edge, hugging the trail. He couldn't have fallen too far away. She followed the skid marks down the ravine. Matt lay against a rock on a steep incline. A nasty gash bled on his forehead. "We've got to get down to him."

Matt's audio guy waved his cell phone. "I'll call for help."

"And in the meantime, do the rest of you just plan to

stand around and wait?" she asked. If only she had Zack and Ryan with her. They would help.

Her camera guy Ernie shrugged. "The race is still going, Millie. You're in first place."

First place.

It's what she'd wanted. It's what she'd set out to do for the students at her school.

All Millie had to do was continue up the path, step on the mat and collect her check. And she'd do that knowing Matt was alone and injured. What if he didn't wake up? What if he woke up and moved the wrong way? He could fall further down the steep slope.

She heard a groan. "Matt?"

"Down here."

"I'm coming down."

"No, Millie," Matt yelled. "The race."

"You could pass out again."

"I won't." His voice sounded weak. "Run, Millie. Win."

She glanced at the trail, at her dream lying at the finish line. But, she realized, that wasn't her dream any longer. At the end of the day winning the race wasn't going to change who she was. Running the race had done that. "I already won."

"But your plans... Your kids—"

"I've come a long way since San Francisco." Cautiously Millie stepped off the trail, feeling her way, grasping at rocks and fallen trees to slow her descent. "I can make other plans. My students will understand I had to make the right choice."

The only choice she could make and still live with herself.

As she scrambled down the steep incline, her boots slid on the rocks and slippery soil, but she made it. "Hey."

The corners of his mouth curved. "I knew you had a thing for me, Millie. Otherwise why would you give up your chance at a million dollars?"

"I'm a sucker for a pretty face."

"Me, too." He blinked. "That's why I like you."

He had cuts on his face and arms, but Millie couldn't tell if he'd broken anything. "What hurts?"

"My head. I really blew it."

"Don't worry about the race," she said. "Does anything else hurt?"

"Nope." He straightened. "Help me up."

Millie's first-aid training kicked in. So did common sense. "Are you sure that's a good idea?"

"Nothing's broken. Probably a concussion," Matt said. "I'm a paramedic, remember?"

"I remember."

His brown eyes pleaded with her. "I gotta finish the race."

"I know." She placed her arm around him and helped him up. He weighed a lot more than she imagined. All that muscle, no doubt. He stood for a moment then sat, pulling her down with him. "Matt?"

His eyelids closed. "Give me a minute."

"Open your eyes." She used her harshest I'm-going-to-send-you-to-the-principal's-office tone. "Now."

He opened them. Thank goodness.

But now what? Millie wasn't going to be able to get him out of here by herself. She called up to Matt's camera crew, who had been joined by Bert and Ernie and seemed to be having some kind of argument.

"Hey!" she yelled. "Can you give us a hand down here?"

The men paused. Shuffled.

"Help's on the way," one of them called back finally.

Millie looked at Matt, trying to hide her irritation for his sake. "Hear that? Help is coming."

"I don't need help," he said softly. "I have you."

She appreciated the voice of confidence, but what she wouldn't give for someone big and strong to come down the side of the hill before Matt lost consciousness again.

"Yo dudes," Derek yelled. "What are you doing down there? Making out?"

She glanced up to see Derek and three film crews peering down from the trail. "Matt fell. Help us up."

"Help you—"

"Please, Derek."

Derek shook his head slowly. "No can do, Millie babe."

"But...Matt's your friend."

"He was my teammate," Derek said, taking a step back. "He hasn't been my friend in years. But I'm glad he's your friend because that just earned me a million bucks even with this bum knee. I fell, too, and no one helped me."

"Sorry, Millie," Matt whispered.

"Don't be sorry," she said. "I'm right where I should be."

Winning a million dollars would have helped the students at her school, but she still had to live with the choices she made during the race. There was always...Plan B.

As for her father, well... Pleasing him might not ever happen and that was finally okay. She'd done her best. That's all she could have hoped to do.

Millie defined success differently than her father, and if he couldn't accept her as she was, so be it. She was proud of what she was doing with her life, what she'd accomplished so far. She wouldn't let him make her feel bad about herself again.

More steam poured from Mount Saint Helens.

Millie sat next to Matt. "I don't think I can pull you up myself."

He grimaced. "I've got to finish the race, Millie."

"With a concussion?"

"So I won't run. But I need to get up this cliff. If they haul me out of here, I'm out of the race."

"The race isn't as important as your health."

"It is to me. I've come this far. I want to finish." His eyes met hers with a determination equaling her own. "Help me."

She drew a deep breath. She wanted to help. But—

"Millie!" Jace's voice, sharp with fear, carried down the side of the mountain. "Are you all right?"

Relief flooded her. She stood, craning her neck to look up the cliff. Jace leaned over the edge, looking at her with intense, dark eyes.

"I'm fine."

"Then what are you doing down there?" he asked.

"Matt fell," she explained. "He hit his head."

"Is he going to make it?"

"Yes. His camera crew called for help. But..."

"What?"

"He wants to finish the race. I can't get him back to the trail by myself."

"Where's Derek?" Jace asked.

The race. That's all he cared about.

Millie shouldn't be disappointed. Jace had his priorities and she had hers. They didn't match. Still, she felt like she'd been hit in the stomach with one of the broken, battered sun-bleached trees.

"He's got about a two-minute lead on you, but he's got a bum knee," Millie called up, proud of the steadiness of her voice. "You can catch him and win. Run, Jace." She turned away. "It's what you're good at anyway."

With that, she sat back down, her heart aching more than she thought possible.

Matt regarded her with deep, sympathetic eyes. "You okay?"

No. She forced a smile anyway. "I will be as soon as we figure out how to get you out of here."

You can catch him and win.

The words reverberated in his head. He wanted to win. Derek was injured. All Jace had to do was run.

Millie was fine. Matt was fine—or he would be once help arrived. Jace had no reason to stay.

She had sacrificed her chance to win to stay with Matt.

The realization sat in Jace's stomach like lead and weighted his feet to the ground.

He glared at the three production crews, standing around filming. "Why aren't you getting them the hell out of there? Matt's hurt."

And Millie, who deserved to win, was stuck down there with him. But, Jace realized, she would have been down there no matter who had fallen. A fellow racer, a crew member, a total stranger. That's who Millie was and what she did.

"Hey, I called for help," Matt's audio guy said.

Zack shouldered his camera. "It's the show, Jace. We all have our jobs to do. Yours is to run."

Run, Jace. Millie's soft voice haunted him. *It's what you're good at anyway.*

He couldn't move. She was right. He'd always run away. Until she came into his life.

She hadn't let him run away. She'd challenged him.

She'd demanded the best from him, and he'd given it to her. Or had. Until his fear got in the way.

He'd been running since he was eight years old, ever since his father had left. Millie gave him a reason to stand still. To stop reaching for what came next and finally live. Now.

Jace couldn't go back and change the past, but he wasn't about to make the same mistake. Everything he knew about her, everything they had experienced as teammates, showed him they belonged together. She might not think so, but he was willing to take that chance.

He couldn't leave her again. Not even for a million dollars.

Another burst of steam spewed from the crater. "You up for another try?" Millie asked Matt.

"If you are," he said. "I don't want you to hurt yourself."

"I'll be fine."

And Millie would be. She'd taken chances. She'd risked her heart. And even though the ending hadn't turned out like she'd hoped, Millie would do it again.

Not tomorrow. Not anytime soon.

But someday.

Rocks tumbled down the slope. Had help arrived?

She turned.

And saw Jace, sliding down the slope toward them, his blue clothes covered with ash and his face determined.

Her heart—her poor, foolish heart—leaped.

"What are you doing down here?"

His gaze held hers. "I'm not leaving my teammate."

Her breath caught. "But…the race."

Jace shrugged.

She'd wanted to believe… She'd wanted to hope…

Her insides tingled. He hadn't let her down. Helping Matt had been more important than the money.

"Thanks, dude," Matt said.

"That's some cut." Jace kneeled next to Matt. "But you're going to have to come up with something better the next time you want to be alone with Millie."

"Funny guy. I'd laugh," Matt said, "but it would hurt too much."

"Come on, Freckles." Jace winked. "Let's get this bad boy out of here."

"Jace." Her voice cracked.

"What?"

Emotion threatened to overwhelm her. "Thank you."

Together she and Jace struggled to bring Matt up the steep incline. Zack and Ryan put down their equipment and helped. With four of them, they were able to get Matt back on the trail.

"The emergency response team will be here soon," Matt's camera guy said.

"He needs to finish the race first," Millie explained.

Jace shot her a questioning glance.

"You go," she said, loving him. Wanting him to win. "We'll be fine."

"I'm not leaving you again," he said.

And this time, she believed him.

"Come on." He put a supporting arm around Matt. "Let's get this show on the road."

The three of them made their way up the trail with two camera crews ahead of them and another, Zack and Ryan, behind them.

It was a long and slow and tiring trek, but Millie wouldn't have had it any other way. She saw the dome building on the volcano. Suddenly pieces broke off and tumbled down. "Look at that."

"Amazing," Jace said.

Millie nodded. "Everything about this race has been amazing."

They reached the Johnston Ridge Observatory that was built into the side of a mountain. People milled about on the first of two viewing decks. A third, with the finish line, was below them. A familiar looking *Cash Around the Globe* banner fluttered in the breeze.

Excitement lifted her fatigue. "There's the finish line."

Jace removed his arm from Matt's shoulders. "Can you make it the rest of the way?"

"Yeah. I want to finish on my own two feet," Matt said. "You two go ahead."

"Are you sure, Matt?" she asked anxiously.

"Sure." His eyes met Jace's in masculine understanding. "Go, man. Run."

"I'm not running anymore." Jace clasped his hand to hers. Millie's heart pounded. "Can you guys give us a minute?"

Matt smiled with wry resignation. "You're determined to win the real prize, aren't you?"

"Yes," Jace said.

"Right. Well, then, I'm out of here." He limped away, followed by his camera crew.

"Go on," Jace said to the remaining film crews. "Show's over."

"Are you kidding?" Ryan asked.

"No way, man," Zack said. "This is through-the-roof ratings stuff."

"Why not?" Jace muttered.

The crew grinned.

Millie stared at him. "I know what you gave up to stop racing to help Matt."

"I didn't stop racing for Matt," Jace said. "I stopped racing for you."

"Me?"

"Yes, you, Freckles."

Millie wanted to hope; she wanted to believe things could be different between them. She wasn't about to let the chance pass her by. "Then why did you choose to race alone?"

"Someone I know once told me I was afraid, but I didn't believe her," he explained. "Turns out she was right. I realized I needed to be brave like her and stop running away."

"What changed?"

"You." He caressed her face. "You're a very special woman, Millie Kincaid."

She forced herself to breathe. "Special like a teammate or friend?"

"That's not what I was thinking."

"What were you thinking?" she asked.

"You want me to spell it out."

She tilted her chin. "Yes."

"Okay." He laughed. "You're strong, gutsy, smart. I've never met anyone nicer, more nurturing or generous. You care about everyone. You act so serious sometimes, yet you can be as playful as a kitten. You might be shy at times, but confidence radiates from you."

Her heart overflowed with joy.

"Do you want me to go on?" he asked.

"That's enough. For now."

"There is something else I want to say."

"What?" she asked.

"You taught me to stop chasing the material prize. To

forget about the appearance of success and want the real thing." He took her hand. "You are the real thing. And, I love you."

The air whooshed from her lungs.

"I love you, Millie Kincaid." He took her hands in his. "I fell in love with you during *The Groom*, but I was too scared to realize it. I've spent my entire life taking care of people. Then you come along. I thought you needed to be taken care of, too, but I was wrong. You can take care of yourself just fine."

"That's because you taught me to believe in myself," she admitted. "All those things we did during the race. Having you there to cheer me on helped me overcome my fears, gain confidence and trust again."

He brushed his lips across hers.

"You made me realize I've been taking care of everybody because I wanted to be needed. But really all I needed was to be loved." He looked at her with a kind of self-deprecating smile. "Now I know what it feels like to risk rejection on national television."

"What are you talking about?" she asked.

He got down on one knee. "Marry me, Millie. Be my wife and the mother of my children. Please."

Elation bubbled inside her.

Jace Westfall had once been the last man on Earth she'd wanted to see again or talk to, but now he was the only man on Earth she needed. The only man she could picture herself spending the rest of her life with. The only man she loved.

"Yes." She threw her arms around him. "Yes, I will marry you. I love you."

Jace rose. He kissed her long and hard.

Millie hoped he always kissed her with such hunger and

passion. She heard clapping and pulled away. "That must be our cue."

"Ready, Freckles?" he asked.

Millie nodded. Zack moved closer to them, but she didn't care. What she had with Jace was real. Being on camera wouldn't change that. Nothing could.

Jace laced his fingers with hers. Together, with Zack and Ryan, they walked down to the observatory platform. Colt and the other racers, minus the pink team, stood on either side of the finish mat.

Jace and Millie jumped on the mat at the same time.

"Millie and Jace," Colt said. "You are third."

"Who cares what place we finished." Jace laughed. "We won the best prize of all."

Colt stared at them with a puzzled expression in his eyes. "What prize is that?"

Leaning into Jace, soaking up his warmth and strength, Millie grinned. "Each other."

* * * * *

Kimberley Blackstone didn't notice the waiting horde of media until it was too late. Flashbulbs exploded around her like a New Year's light show. She skidded to a halt, so abruptly her trailing suitcase all but overtook her.

This had to be a case of mistaken identity. Surely. Kimberley hadn't been on the paparazzi hit list for close to a decade, not since she'd estranged herself from her billionaire father and his headline-hungry diamond business.

But no, it was *her* name they called. *Her* face was the focus of a swarm of lenses that circled her like avid hornets. Her heart started to pound with fear-fueled adrenaline.

What did they want?

What was going on?

With a rising sense of bewilderment she scanned the crowd for a clue, and her gaze fastened on a tall, leonine figure forcing his way to the front. A tall, familiar figure. Her head came up in stunned recognition, and their gazes collided across the sea of heads before the cameras erupted with another barrage of flashes, this time right in her exposed face.

Blinded by the flashbulbs—and by the shock of that momentary eye-meet—Kimberley didn't realize his intent until he'd forged his way to her side, possibly by the sheer strength of his personality. She felt his arm wrap around her shoulder, pulling her into the protective shelter of his body, allowing her no time to object. No chance to lift her hands to ward him off.

In the space of a hastily drawn breath, she found herself plastered knee-to-nose against six feet two inches of hard-bodied male.

Ric Perrini.

Her lover for ten torrid weeks, her husband for ten tumultuous days.

Her ex for ten tranquil years.

After all this time, he should not have felt so familiar but, oh dear, he did. She knew the scent of that body and its lean, muscular strength. She knew its heat and its slick power and every response it could draw from hers.

She also recognized the ease with which he'd taken control of the moment and the decisiveness of his deep voice when it rumbled close to her ear. "I have a car waiting outside. Is this your only luggage?"

Kimberley nodded. "I assume you will tell me," she said tightly, "what this welcome party is all about."

"Not while the welcome party is within earshot. No."

Barking a request for the cameramen to stand aside, Perrini took her hand and pulled her into step with his ground-eating stride. Kimberley let him, because he was right, damn his arrogant, Italian-suited hide. Despite the speed with which he whisked her across the airport terminal, she could almost feel the hot breath of the pursuing media on her back.

This was neither the time nor the place for explanations. Inside his car, however, she would get answers.

Now that the initial shock had been blown away—by the haste of their retreat, by the heat of her gathering indignation, by the rush of adrenaline fired by Perrini's presence and the looming verbal battle—her brain was starting to tick over. This had to be her father's doing. And if it was a Howard Blackstone publicity ploy, then it had to be about Blackstone Diamonds, the company that ruled his life.

The knowledge made her chest tighten with a familiar ache of disillusionment.

She'd known her father would be flying in from Sydney for today's opening of the newest in his chain of exclusive, high-end jewelry boutiques. The opulent shopfront sat adjacent to the rival business where Kimberley worked. No coincidence, she thought bitterly, just as it was no coincidence that Ric Perrini was here in Auckland ushering her to his car.

Perrini was Howard Blackstone's right-hand man, second in command at Blackstone Diamonds, a legacy of his short-lived marriage to the boss's daughter. No doubt her father had sent him to fetch her; the question was *why?*

* * * * *

Get swept away down under with the glitz and glamour of the Blackstone empire as Kimberley tries to determine the real reason behind her "reunion" with Ric....

Look for VOWS & A VENGEFUL GROOM
by Bronwyn Jameson,
in stores January 2008.

When Kimberley Blackstone's father is presumed dead, Kimberley is required to take over the helm of Blackstone Diamonds. She has to work closely with her ex, Ric Perrini, to battle not only the press, but also the fierce attraction still sizzling between them. Does Ric feel the same...or is it the power her share of Blackstone Diamonds will provide him as he battles for boardroom supremacy.

Look for

VOWS &
A VENGEFUL GROOM
by
BRONWYN
JAMESON

Available January wherever you buy books

REQUEST YOUR FREE BOOKS!
2 FREE NOVELS PLUS 2
FREE GIFTS!

HARLEQUIN ROMANCE®

From the Heart, For the Heart

YES! Please send me 2 FREE Harlequin Romance® novels and my 2 FREE gifts. After receiving them, if I don't wish to receive any more books, I can return the shipping statement marked "cancel." If I don't cancel, I will receive 4 brand-new novels every month and be billed just $3.57 per book in the U.S., or $4.05 per book in Canada, plus 25¢ shipping and handling per book and applicable taxes, if any*. That's a savings of over 15% off the cover price! I understand that accepting the 2 free books and gifts places me under no obligation to buy anything. I can always return a shipment and cancel at any time. Even if I never buy another book from Harlequin, the two free books and gifts are mine to keep forever.

114 HDN EEV7   314 HDN EEWK

Name	(PLEASE PRINT)
Address	Apt.
City	State/Prov.	Zip/Postal Code

Signature (if under 18, a parent or guardian must sign)

Mail to the **Harlequin Reader Service®**:
IN U.S.A.: P.O. Box 1867, Buffalo, NY 14240-1867
IN CANADA: P.O. Box 609, Fort Erie, Ontario L2A 5X3

Not valid to current Harlequin Romance subscribers.

Want to try two free books from another line?
Call 1-800-873-8635 or visit www.morefreebooks.com.

* Terms and prices subject to change without notice. NY residents add applicable sales tax. Canadian residents will be charged applicable provincial taxes and GST. This offer is limited to one order per household. All orders subject to approval. Credit or debit balances in a customer's account(s) may be offset by any other outstanding balance owed by or to the customer. Please allow 4 to 6 weeks for delivery.

Your Privacy: Harlequin is committed to protecting your privacy. Our Privacy Policy is available online at www.eHarlequin.com or upon request from the Reader Service. From time to time we make our lists of customers available to reputable firms who may have a product or service of interest to you. If you would prefer we not share your name and address, please check here. ☐

HR07

Coming Next Month

**Start your New Year with a bang with six terrific reads,
only from Harlequin Romance®.**

#3997 HER HAND IN MARRIAGE Jessica Steele
Get ready for the perfect English gentleman to sweep you off your feet!
Romillie never imagined that a high-flying executive like Naylor would
be interested in an ordinary girl like her, but she's bowled over when he
whisks her away to his beautiful Cotswold cottage....

#3998 THE RANCHER'S DOORSTEP BABY Patricia Thayer
Western Weddings
Does the image of a man cradling a tiny baby in his arms melt your heart?
You aren't alone! Rachel isn't sure whether drifter Cole will stick around for
long, but seeing the tender way he holds her delicate baby, she knows her
heart belongs to him forever.

#3999 THE SHEIKH'S UNSUITABLE BRIDE Liz Fielding
Desert Brides
Have you ever wanted someone you really shouldn't have? Desert prince
Zahir knows Diana is not what his family and country expect in a wife. But
this thoroughly unsuitable woman, whose eyes sparkle with mischief, is
worth breaking the rules for.

#4000 THE BRIDESMAID'S BEST MAN Barbara Hannay
One special night between rugged best man Mark and beautiful
bridesmaid Sophie seemed to be all they would get to share, as Mark had
to return home to Australia. But now it seems these two will be sharing the
most special job of all—parenthood!

#4001 MOONLIGHT AND ROSES Jackie Braun
Jaye thought she knew what she wanted from life—her career, and the
freedom to be her own woman. But the intoxicating mix of new business
partner Zack, the glimmer of moonlight and the scent of roses in the air is
making her change her mind....

#4002 A MOTHER IN A MILLION Melissa James
Heart to Heart
How can you be sure that someone loves you—really loves *you*?
Jennifer's heart goes out to single dad Noah and his motherless children,
but when he proposes, Jennifer wants to be sure he wants her as his wife,
not just as a mother to his children.

HRCNM1207